A HOLIDAY ROMANCE
OF THE UNNATURAL BRETHREN

BLOOD AND MISTLETOE

USA TODAY BESTSELLING AUTHOR

SILVANA G. SÁNCHEZ

*To those who believe "Winter Wonderland"
should include at least three supernatural species*

The night is darkening round me,
The wild winds coldly blow;
But a tyrant spell has bound me,
And I cannot, cannot go.

— EMILY BRONTË

MY FREE AUDIOBOOKS

Do you like FREE audiobooks?
Go check out my YouTube channel!
Subscribe and get notified when new books are up!

My darling darklings,

Blood and Mistletoe provides a glimpse into the Unnatural Brethren's extended world one week after the events in *Cast in Blood* and *Embers of Fate*.

Reading those prior installments is highly recommended to fully appreciate this brief yet meaningful visit with our beloved characters during the magical season of Yule.

It is my hope that you find joy in spending a little more time with the lethal immortals, cunning witches, and fierce shifters who feel like family, as I work on the next full-length novels coming soon.

While I toil away writing *Blood of the Ancient, Blood of the Viking,* and *Wings of Shadow,* may this short story warm your heart and spark your holiday spirit.

As always, thank you for your continued support and enthusiasm for these characters' interwoven journeys. Your passion makes the long hours and late nights of writing worth every minute.

Now brew some tea, cozy up with a blanket, and let this tale of forbidden bonds, unrestrained desire, and the mysterious spirits of Yule envelop you.

Happy reading!

Yours in the shadowy season,
Silvana.

BLOOD AND MISTLETOE

This Yule, love answers mistletoe's call

Power has a price. For Cassandra Deveraux, it's paid in bear magic and broken promises, sealed with a brand that makes her blood sing even as her heart rebels. But this Yule holds more dangers than navigating her forced bond with the Ursa King. A secret grows within her—one that could shatter the delicate balance between supernatural factions.

As the first formal dinner at Draken Manor approaches, ancient magics stir. The Last Dragon Shifter's frost-laden halls become a crucible where vampire blood meets witch magic, where bear's strength tests dragon fire. For Cassandra, maintaining the facade of being merely Gavriil's branded mate becomes impossible as her power spirals beyond control.

But when a child's innocent magic calls forth the true power of mistletoe—a force that once bound supernatural peace treaties—enemies and allies alike must choose: hold to old grudges or embrace the possibility of new bonds forged in winter's heart.

BLOOD AND MISTLETOE

IVAN LOCKHART

Season greetings, my beloved darklings,

Have you missed me? Oh, I've missed you. Terribly.

The crisp air carries a distinct stillness as another year nears its end. For a brooding immortal like myself, the passage of time bears little consequence, yet the enchantment of your fleeting mortal lives provides curious intrigue.

But how do supernatural creatures like myself spend the holidays? You may wonder.

Consider this brief tale a furtive glance into the shadows that permeate my perilous world. Dangerous secrets and lethal desires lurk beneath even the most innocuous surface. Tread carefully, for true terror hides itself in beauty.

Now then. Time carries on, and precious moments slip away. Lose yourself in the holidays' charm, but not so completely that you forget what lurks in the darkness. My world can prove more treacherous than what your mind may fathom.

For your loyalty, I thank you. For your discretion, I trust you. And for your forbidden allure... I thirst everlastingly.

Yours in lethal eternity,

Ivan Lockhart

CASSANDRA

*P*ower has a price. Mine was paid in bear magic and broken promises, sealed with a brand that makes my blood sing even as my heart rebels.

Magic crackles in the portrait gallery, making the gilded frames tremor as I storm past generations of Deveraux witches. Their painted eyes follow my furious stride, perhaps wondering how their precious bloodline has come to this—their heiress, branded like cattle by the Ursa King.

"Do not walk away from me." Gavriil's voice carries that edge of command that makes the mark beneath my skin burn hotter. His footsteps echo on marble, unhurried, confident. He knows I have nowhere to run.

I halt before Juliette's portrait, my fingers curling into fists as I stare up at her serene expression. Even in oil paint, her deep green eyes hold countless secrets. Did she know this would happen when she arranged my match with the Ursa King? Did she foresee the way his magic would crawl through my veins like poison?

"I said… stop." Closer now. The air grows thick with his presence, that damned blend of cedar and smoke that makes my head spin.

My fingers trace the ancient carvings in the doorframe—mistletoe and holly intertwined, symbols of power older than the Deveraux line itself. Even now, with his brand burning beneath my skin, I feel the old magic respond to my touch.

"Or what?" I whirl to face him, satisfaction flaring as he stops short. "You'll add another layer to your spell? Brand me twice?"

His dark eyes ignite with spectral blue flames, burning low with pride and steady assurance. The shadows around us deepen, responding to his rising power. Even in his tailored black suit, there's no mistaking the predator beneath—the bear king who always gets what he wants.

"You still don't understand what I've given you."

He steps closer, and despite every instinct screaming to retreat, I hold my ground. "This gift—"

"Gift?" The word tastes like ash. A nearby vase shatters, water and roses spilling across priceless marble. "You call this magical leash a *gift?*"

His hand shoots out, fingers wrapping around my wrist. The touch sends electricity racing up my arm, his brand recognizing its master. But something else stirs beneath my skin—a wild, untamed energy that has nothing to do with his spell.

"Feel that?" His voice drops lower, rough with desire and triumph. "Your magic responds to mine. Fighting it only makes the connection stronger."

I wrench away from his grip and push through the study doors, my heart thundering against my ribs. But he follows, his presence filling the room like smoke, suffocating.

The hearth roars to life, flames leaping high as my control slips further. Outside, snow falls in thick flurries, obscuring the grounds of Deveraux Manor. The soft moonlight filtering through the windows casts Gavriil in shadows and gold, highlighting the sharp planes of his face, the fierce gleam in his eyes.

"You cannot fight this forever, printsessa." His voice carries that damned sensual edge that sets my nerves on fire. "The more you resist, the stronger my spell becomes."

"Watch me." I step back, but the massive oak desk prevents my retreat.

The Ursa King, unwilling to lose this fight, inches closer. "Your defiance..." He reaches out, bold fingers brushing my cheek. The touch sends jolts of electricity through my body, his brand responding to his proximity. "It only makes you more captivating. The bear in me thrives at the challenge."

Something snaps inside me. Warmth courses through my being, fast and devastating as a fearsome tidal wave—overwhelming, unlike any sensation I've experienced before.

My shoulders jolt as the crystal decanter on the desk explodes, sending shards and cognac flying. The chandelier above us creaks, then begins to swing, its lights flickering wildly before the bulbs shatter one by one.

Darkness descends, broken only by the hearth's fluttering glow and the violet flames that surely now burn in my eyes—a mirror of his spectral blue ones.

"Fascinating." Gavriil doesn't flinch as my magic whips around us like a tempest. If anything, his smile turns wider. "My branding spell flows mysteriously within you. Its magic grows stronger by the day."

I want to scream that he has no idea, that the power rushing through me has nothing to do with his spell and *everything* to do with the life growing inside me—Dristan's child, a secret that burns hotter than any spell or incantation. I could speak of the sudden shift in my magic that started scarce days ago; subtle tremors in my surroundings at first. How its strength and frequency have only increased ever since... I could tell him all these things, but instead, I bite my tongue until I taste copper.

The remaining lights in the room buzz dangerously, their pulse matching the erratic rhythm of my heart. Papers scatter from the desk in a macabre dance, and I watch them with a strange detachment, as if floating above my own body. Locks of my raven hair brush against my cheeks, swept in the magical maelstrom of my untamed power, each strand charged with energy that makes my skin prickle.

My throat constricts, lungs burning as I struggle to draw breath. The air itself seems to thicken, heavy with power that no longer answers to my will. Through the roaring in my ears, I hear the windows shudder—or perhaps that's my own body trembling as reality warps around me. When they creak, a sound like splintering fate, I shut my eyes against the inevitable, my chest so tight it feels like iron bands are crushing my ribs.

The scene unfolds before my closed lids like a waking nightmare—my own form wreathed in violent light, magic spiraling out of control, while I remain trapped, both participant and witness to my undoing.

For a moment, raw dread flashes across Gavriil's face—not of me, but *for* me. His hands grip my shoulders, steadying.

"Breathe, Cassandra." His voice drops lower, gentler. "You need to contain this before…"

An antique letter opener flies from the desk; it spears through the air, missing his head by inches. He doesn't even blink.

"Before what?" I challenge, even as my knees threaten to buckle. The magic is too much, too wild. "Before I reveal to our world what a mistake you made in choosing me?"

His laugh is dark honey and winter's fury. "Oh, printsessa. You have no idea what you're capable of." He pulls me closer, one hand cupping my face. "But I do. And soon, everyone else will see it too."

The envelope in his other hand catches my eye— heavy cream paper bearing the Draken's seal. An invitation that promises to change everything in our world.

Power rips through me like a tidal wave, wild magic writhing beneath my skin in search of release. The cream envelope in Gavriil's hand seems to mock me with its elegance, promise of more politics, pretense, and nights spent fighting his brand's magnetic pull.

"Nikolaas Draken," I manage through clenched teeth, "is hosting a Yule dinner."

"And we shall attend," he adds, impossibly cool and collected. Gavriil's thumb traces my jawline, his touch sending fresh sparks of lightning through my overtaxed nerves. "Together."

The last word hangs between us like frost in still air. *Together*. As if we're truly mates rather than pawns in this supernatural game of chess. As if his magical brand hasn't forced on us this facade of unity.

"What if I refuse?" Even as I say it, I know it's futile. The brand pulses beneath my skin, an unwelcomed reminder of my gilded cage.

His other hand settles on my waist, and damn him, but my body leans into his touch like a flower seeking sunlight. "You won't." His absolute certainty sets my teeth on edge. "You're a Deveraux witch. You understand the importance of maintaining appearances."

A bitter laugh escapes my lips. "Appearances?" The remaining lights in the study flicker dangerously. "Is that what we're calling this elaborate charade?"

"This is no charade, printsessa." His grip tightens, both possessive and protective as another wave of uncontrolled magic rolls through the room. "You're *mine* now. The sooner you accept that truth—"

"I will never be yours." The words emerge as a growl, but beneath my defiance lies true fear. Not of him, but of the wild power surging through me, growing stronger each day.

His eyes narrow, spectral flames dancing in their depths. "Mm. We shall see." He releases me and steps back, but the searing heat of his touch lingers. "The dinner is in three days. I'll send a car."

It's expected. This isn't just any dinner, but the inaugural event thrown by the Last Dragon Shifter. It's not only Nik's chance to officially declare his upcoming rise as alpha, but also an important moment for the Ursa King to make our first appearance in the supernatural world. We'll present a united front that will surprise and impress both our friends and enemies alike.

As he turns to leave, another surge of magic rips

through my being. Behind me, the studio's heavy drapes catch fire, flames racing up the fabric with supernatural speed. Gavriil waves his hand almost lazily, extinguishing the blaze with his own power within seconds.

"Oh, and Cassandra?" He pauses at the doorway, his silhouette carved in shadows and dying firelight. "Work on your control. We wouldn't want any... accidents at the Draken's gathering."

The doors close behind him with a soft click that sounds like a prison cell engaging. I sink into the nearest chair, my hands trembling as I press them against my still-flat stomach.

My vision blurs with forthcoming tears. Exhaustion and grief tangle in my heart. These outbursts of magic are taking a greater toll on me each time they come.

Three days. I have three days to learn to control this escalating power before I'm thrust into a room full of supernatural creatures who can sense magic. Three days to perfect the lie that I am simply Gavriil's branded mate, nothing more.

The invitation lies abandoned on the desk, Nikolaas' seal gleaming like fresh blood in the firelight.

I can almost hear Fate laughing.

2

IVAN

The City of Lights fails to live up to its name tonight. Grey clouds hang low over Paris, heavy with the threat of snow. Meanwhile, I balance atop an antique ladder in my lair's grand salon, weaving pine branches through the crystal chandelier like some Martha Stewart wannabe. The things I do for love.

My top-of-the-line Sonos—because immortality is no excuse for dated tech—fills the space with a crystal-clear rendition of "Auld Lang Syne." Billie Holiday's version, because if I'm going to indulge in melancholy, I might as well do it with style.

"A little to the left," Juliette says from her perch on the velvet settee. Her violet eyes sparkle with amusement as she sips mulled wine.

I shift the branch a fraction of an inch, grinding my teeth. "Better?" I'm obliged to ask. Three hundred and fifty years of immortal life, and here I am, taking interior decorating advice from a witch who spent the last three centuries dead.

"The mistletoe doesn't belong with common pine." Her voice carries that familiar edge of ancient knowledge as she sets down her wine. Juliette's amethyst eyes gleam with the same look she gets before unleashing some time-worn secret. "Our kind has forgotten so much—how the Unnatural Brethren used to gather beneath winter's white berries, where no blood could be spilled, no magic could harm. Even the most vicious supernatural creatures had to lay down arms under mistletoe's blessing."

I arch an eyebrow, unable to resist teasing her. "And here I thought it was just for stealing kisses."

"Every tradition has its roots in power, my love." She traces a pattern in the air, and I feel the old magic stir around us. "Mistletoe bridges worlds—death and life, peace and war. It remembers what we've forgotten, recognizes blood and bone and magic older than any of our current alliances."

I crack half a smile, partly showing my fangs. "Is that why you're making me hang every sprig in the flat?" I purr. *"Old magic?"*

"Would you prefer I tell you it's because I enjoy watching you balance on stepladders?" she counters, each sassy word delighting my senses.

I step down, brushing pine needles from my sleeve. The mistletoe hangs above us now, pearl-white berries catching candlelight like stars. For a moment, the air thickens with old magic—the kind that remembers when these plants were more than simple decorations, when they held the power to bind peace or break worlds. But before I can follow that unsettling thought, Juliette moves.

"Perfect." She rises from the seat and glides across the room, her silk dressing gown rustling with each step. Her delicate arms slip around my waist, and she presses a kiss between my shoulder blades. The simple touch ignites every nerve ending in my body. "Thank you for indulging me."

"Well," I turn to face her, pulling her closer, "someone has to maintain standards around here. God knows Jon would never let us hear the end of it if our Yule decorations weren't up to par with Deveraux Manor's."

Her laughter, rich and warm as the wine in her glass, fills the room. But there's an edge to it, a slight tremor that betrays her concern. We're both thinking of Cassandra, of the magical whirlwind recently gathering beneath her skin.

"She's getting worse, isn't she?" I ask, though I already know the answer. I've seen how the streetlights flicker when she passes, how wine glasses crack in her presence, how the very air seems to bend around her these days.

Juliette's expression darkens. "The child grows stronger each day. And with it, her powers..." She drifts to the window, watching as the first snowflakes begin to fall. "I fear what might happen at Nikolaas' dinner."

"Surely, Gavriil's brand—"

"The brand may be the only thing keeping her magic contained at all." She turns back to me, and for a moment, I glimpse the emotional burden of centuries in her eyes. "Though she doesn't realize it yet."

I move to the drink cart, pouring myself a generous measure of blood-laced bourbon. The crystal decanter catches the firelight, casting crimson shadows across my hands. "I should take her shopping tomorrow," I say, the words forming before I've fully thought them through. "Get her mind off things. Maybe help her find something suitably impressive to wear to this circus Nikolaas is arranging."

"Playing fairy godfather, are we?" Juliette's lips curl into a knowing smile.

"Please." I roll my eyes, taking a long sip. "I simply refuse to let any goddaughter of mine show up to a supernatural gathering looking anything less than lethal. Besides," I add, more softly, "someone needs to watch over her."

"*Goddaughter*, huh?" she asks, raising a teasing eyebrow.

"Don't look at me like that," I mumble, waving a hand dismissively. "You started this with the fairy thing. It's just a manner of speech…"

Juliette gives no answer, but her knowing gaze speaks volumes.

"Oh, alright. I *do* care about her," I finally concede. "She's my favorite Deveraux witch—after you, of course."

"My brave, handsome man." Juliette comes to me again, taking the glass from my hand and setting it aside. "Always protecting everyone else, even on Yule."

"Speaking of ancient protections," I say, drawing her flush against me. My fingers trace the curve of her spine, following paths older than memory. "I believe there's another mistletoe tradition worth honoring."

A smile curves my lips as I glance up at the white berries gleaming above us. "One that speaks less of supernatural treaties and more of... sealed bargains."

Her violet eyes dance with both amusement and understanding. We both know the deeper meaning of mistletoe—how it once bound enemies in temporary peace, how it still remembers the old ways of making promises between powerful beings. But right now, with her warm and willing in my arms, I'm far more interested in its modern implications.

"Such a clever vampire," she murmurs, "finding loopholes in ancient laws." Her fingers curl into my shirt, and I feel the tremor in them—not fear, but that exquisite tension between power and desire. Above us, the mistletoe gleams with knowing light, witness to pacts made in shadow and sealed with a kiss.

"Only the pleasurable ones," I murmur against her throat, where her pulse flutters like bat wings in the dark.

Her laugh turns to a gasp as I trail kisses down her neck, but even as I lose myself in her embrace, part of me remains alert, watching the falling snow and wondering how long we have before this perfect moment shatters like everything else in Cassandra's presence.

3

IVAN

The winter sun hangs low over Champs-Élysées as I escort Cassandra through the holiday crowds. Mortals bustle past with their paper shopping bags and mundane concerns, blissfully unaware of the magical havoc walking among them. Their festive cheer grates on my nerves almost as much as the insipid Christmas carols drifting from every boutique.

"You're scowling again," Cassandra says, linking her arm through mine. "People will think you hate Christmas."

"I *do* hate Christmas." I guide her around a group of tourists gawking at window displays. "All that forced joy and commercialized cheer. Now Yule, that's a proper holiday. Blood sacrifices, wild hunts, orgies in the woods..."

She snorts, a most unladylike sound that would make Juliette wince. "Since when do you participate in orgies?"

"I'll have you know I was quite the libertine in my day," I tease—but not really. We pause before Chanel's window, where a dress of midnight blue silk catches her eye. Perfect for making a certain Ursa King lose his carefully maintained control. "The eighteenth century was a *wild* time."

The light above us flickers, and I feel Cassandra stiffen. Her magic ripples through the air like heat waves off summer pavement. Without missing a beat, I steer her into the boutique before she can shatter every window on the street.

Inside, the shop assistant's maroon eyes glaze slightly as I exert just enough vampire influence to ensure we won't be disturbed. Cassandra notices, of course. She notices everything these days.

"You don't have to keep protecting me," she whispers, running her fingers over silk and lace. "I'm not going to explode."

"God, I hope not. I just got these from Santoni," I muse as I examine my pair of devastatingly expensive shoes. "Perhaps we could avoid testing that theory in the middle of Paris's shopping district?"

She starts to retort, but her words die in her throat as she catches our reflection in the gilt-framed mirror. Next to my eternally twenty-six-year-old face, she looks impossibly young and terrifyingly powerful. Violet flames dance in her eyes, turning grey to bright amethyst—a sure sign her magic is building to dangerous levels.

"Breathe," I tell her, moving to block her from view. "Focus on something solid. The silk under your fingers, the floor beneath your feet..."

"I can't." Her voice breaks. "It's too much. Everything's too much lately."

I take her trembling hands in mine, letting the preternatural chill of my immortal flesh ground her. "I know, little witch. I know." The lights overhead buzz ominously. "But you're stronger than this magic. Stronger than his wretched brand. Stronger than all of it."

Her storm-grey eyes meet mine, and for a moment I see the scared young woman beneath the powerful witch, the one who reminds me so much of Juliette at that age. Then she takes a deep breath, and the violet flames slowly fade.

She remains silent, her gaze distant.

"Look at me," I say, turning her away from the mirror. The violet light recently swirling in her eyes unsettles me, reminds me too much of Juliette, and something else... something older and far more dangerous. "Focus on my voice. Remember who you are."

"A Deveraux witch," she whispers, almost automatically. A crystal perfume bottle on a nearby counter begins to rattle.

"More than that." I guide her toward a rack of evening gowns, strategic movement being preferable to standing still when she's like this. "You're the witch who united the Deveraux lineage. The one who helped bring down the tyrannical rule of Jiao Long. The one who..." I pause, choosing my next words carefully. "The one who won a millenary vampire's heart."

Her breath hitches. The perfume bottle stops shaking.

"Now then," I say, selecting a gown in deep crimson silk. "Let's make sure you're the most devastating creature at this ridiculous dinner. The kind of devastating that makes a certain Ursa King question all his life choices."

A ghost of a smile touches her lips. "You're terrible."

"I'm a vampire, darling. Being terrible is part of my charm." I add a black velvet number to the growing collection in my arms. "Besides, what's the point of attending these tedious gatherings if we can't create a little chaos?"

"Speaking of chaos..." She fingers the delicate beading on one of the dresses. "What do you think he's doing right now?"

I don't have to ask who she means. The question carves into my heart like a wooden stake. *Where are you, Vampire Dad? And why aren't you here when we need you most?*

"Knowing him?" I say instead, forcing lightness into my tone. "Probably brooding in some ancient castle, writing poetry about his immortal angst."

Her laugh is weak but genuine. "I'm not sure that's entirely accurate."

"Sadly, I think it is." I usher her toward the fitting rooms with an armful of silk and promises. "Now, let's get this show going."

4

GAVRIIL

Frost patterns creep across the windows of my study, each crystalline branch a reminder of last winter. *Of her.* Even now, barely a year since her passing, the scent of snow brings back memories of Luciana's laugh, the way her blue eyes would sparkle when the first flakes fell. The wound is still fresh, bleeding at the edges of every thought, turning every holiday tradition into another reminder of her absence.

I tear my gaze from the window and focus on the ancient tome before me. The leather-bound grimoire details every Ursa ritual since our clan's inception. Tradition matters, especially now when the other clans circle like vultures, waiting for any sign of weakness in the alliance between Alexeev and Deveraux.

"Still brooding, brother?"

Samara's voice draws me from my thoughts. She lounges in the doorway, elegant in black silk, a knowing smile playing on her lips. But I catch the concern in her dark eyes—the same look she's worn since that terrible day in Sestroretsk.

"Planning," I correct her, though we both know it's a lie. "Our role in the winter feast needs to be played to perfection."

"Ah yes." She saunters in, trailing her fingers along the bookshelves. "Our first Yule with your chosen mate. Though I notice you don't call her that."

"Don't start."

"I'm merely observing." She drops into the chair across from me, all feline grace and boldness. "The brand is strong, but your heart..." Her gaze drifts to the portrait above the fireplace. Luciana's eyes seem to follow us, painted just days before everything changed.

"My heart is not part of this arrangement." The words emerge colder than intended.

"No," Samara agrees softly. "It lies buried in Russian snow."

Before I can respond, movement in the courtyard catches my eye. Vlad stands in the falling flakes, phone pressed to his ear, his expression soft in a way I rarely see. He must be talking to Anya. My dearest brother, found family when we needed it most, now torn between his loyalty to our clan and the pull of his own—his mate and cub, miles away in Saint Petersburg.

"He misses them terribly," Samara says, following my gaze. "Little Katya grows more beautiful each day, he tells me."

The pride in her voice makes my chest ache. Luciana should be here for this. Our first niece, the next generation of our clan.

"He stays because he must." The word sours in my mouth like tainted blood. Politics and pack loyalty. Chains as strong as any magic. "The other clans would see his departure as weakness."

"And we can't have that." Samara's tone carries a hint of bitterness. "Not when everyone's watching to see if the great Ursa King can truly tame a Deveraux witch."

I close the grimoire with more force than necessary. "Cassandra is not meant to be *tamed*."

"Oh?" My sister's eyebrow arches. "Then what *is* she meant to be?"

The question hangs in the air like frost. What is Cassandra to me? Not love—never that. But something else, something that stirs my magic in ways I hadn't expected. Her defiance awakens the bear inside me, makes my blood sing with the thrill of the hunt. Her power, growing daily beyond even my understanding, both thrills and terrifies.

"She is meant to be exactly what she is," I say finally. "A force of nature wearing human skin." The words freeze between my lips as I stalk to the window.

Beyond the frost-laced glass, Vlad's silhouette blurs in the falling snow, his phone still pressed to his ear, a lifeline to the family he can't join.

"Our union is about power," I add, keeping my tone cool, detached. "About ensuring our clan's survival in a changing world."

"The same way your marriage to Luciana was supposed to be purely political?" Samara's voice carries no judgment, only a gentle irony that pierces deeper than any accusation. She knows how my love for Luciana—a human—shattered every sacred rule our kind holds dear.

I press my forehead against the glass, letting its bitter cold ground me in the present. "That was different," I whisper, watching my breath ghost across the window pane.

"Because you let yourself love her."

"Because she let me be myself." The admission

scrapes my throat raw. "No expectations, no political games. Just... me."

Samara rises, her reflection in the window as graceful as the first light on a winter morning. "And you think Cassandra won't do the same?"

"Cassandra," I say, watching the snow gather on the courtyard stones, "hasn't been given a choice."

Something shifts in my sister's expression. Where once she championed love's triumph over duty, now her eyes hold shadows of harder truths.

"None of us have a choice," I add grimly.

Her fingers press my shoulder, delicate yet steady. "Then it's like you said. We do what we must to survive."

Beyond the glass, Vlad lowers his phone, his shoulders bowing under the weight of separation. In his stance, I see my own grief mirrored—the cost of putting clan before heart, of sacrificing personal happiness for supernatural politics.

"At what cost?" The question tears free before I can cage it. "Look at him, Sam. Look what our survival has cost him."

Samara's silence stretches between us like shadows lengthening at dusk. In the courtyard below, Vlad remains motionless, snow gathering on his shoulders like the weight of responsibilities we've all had to bear.

"We survived Sestroretsk," Sam finally says, her voice barely a whisper. "But survival isn't living, is it?" Her reflection fragments in the frosted glass, overlaying Vlad's distant figure like a double exposure of all we've lost. "Brother, I did not know... When I fought against your match with Cassandra, I thought I was defending love's sanctity. But now, I understand —you're trying to protect us all from worse choices."

My hand presses against the cold window, leaving prints that steam and fade like ghostly signatures. "The other clans circle like wolves in winter, waiting for their moment. One crack in our alliance with the Deverauxs..." The words trail off, heavy with implications.

"And I'm lucky," she continues, a bitter smile playing at her lips. "My dragon prince comes with power enough that none dare challenge our match. But Cassandra—" She stops, the realization blooming in her eyes like winter-pale roses. "You branded her to protect her too, didn't you? Not just to secure the alliance."

The truth of it settles in my chest like ice, sharp and absolute. "The brand marks her as mine. As untouchable. Without it..." Images flash through my mind—other alphas tearing at the Deveraux witch, trying to claim her power for themselves. "Sometimes chains are safer than freedom."

Through the window, I watch Vlad finally turn toward the manor, his face a study of contained grief. In this moment, we're all bound by the same frozen chains—duty, survival, the relentless need to protect what's ours, no matter the cost to our hearts.

I turn away. Samara moves to the hearth, where flames paint shadows across her face like secrets taking form. The fire does little to warm the chill settling in my bones—some frosts simply run too deep.

"The Deveraux line carries ancient magic," I explain, watching her add another log to the flames. Sparks rise like fallen stars seeking heaven. "Cassandra's power..." I pause, remembering how the very air warps around her now, reality bending in ways that set my bear magic on edge. "It's becoming something none of us fully understand."

Samara's fingers trace the carved mistletoe on the mantle, an unconscious gesture that speaks to older spells, older laws. "The other clans sense it too. I've seen how they watch her, their hunger barely concealed behind political smiles." Her hand drops to her side, curling into a fist.

I move to the drink cart, the crystal decanter refracting the light like captured stars. "My brand ensures any challenge to her becomes a challenge to the Ursa throne." Power rumbles beneath my words as I pour two measures of bourbon. "Let them think it's about control, about forcing submission. Better that than having them understand what's really awakening in her blood."

Boot heels click against marble in the corridor—Vlad returning from his call, bringing winter's chill with him. Each step marks time like a heartbeat, counting down to choices we can't escape.

"You fear what she's becoming," Samara observes, accepting the glass I offer. Her voice carries that edge of ancient knowing our bloodline is famous for. "Not for our clan's sake, but for what it might cost her."

Our eyes meet over raised glasses, dark gazes holding secrets older than memory. "Power has a price, sister. And someone always pays it."

5

GAVRIIL

lad enters like winter wind given form, snow still clinging to his dark coat, melting in the study's warmth. His silver eyes catch the flicker of flames as he shrugs off his outer layer, each movement carrying the studied grace of a predator attempting to appear harmless. But I see the tension in his shoulders, the way his fingers flex—unconscious tells that speak of frustration and heartache.

"Are we drinking without me?" He aims for lightness, but something raw edges his voice. "And here I thought we were family."

I pour another measure, watching amber liquid turn alight like trapped sunsets. The bourbon's rich aroma fills the air, mingling with pine smoke and the lingering trace of snow he's brought inside. "We're discussing the upcoming soiree at Draken Manor."

"Ah yes, the dragon's lair." Vlad accepts the glass, a hint of his usual mischief returning. "Tell me, sister, will there be virgin sacrifices and gold-hoarding competitions? Perhaps a wing-spanning contest?"

The color that floods Samara's cheeks stops his teasing cold. Something electric charges the air as Vlad's gaze darts between us, recognition dawning in his eyes like winter sunrise.

"Боги мои." *My gods,* he breathes, his terse tone carrying years of understanding. "This is more serious than I thought. You're actually in love with him."

"Vlad..." Samara's warning comes too late, his name hanging in the air like frost before a storm. The flames paint shadows across her face, unable to hide the truth blazing in her eyes—brighter than any dragon's fire.

"A dragon?" Vlad downs his bourbon in one swift motion. His laugh carries echoes of older hurts, of paths that shaped us all. "Our Sam? The same Sam who once declared all dragons were pompous, gold-obsessed lizards?"

"I was young!" Sam snaps.

"You're *still* young," I interject, earning a glare from my sister.

"People change," she continues, but the words emerge soft, almost reverent. Firelight dances across her features, transforming my fierce sister into someone I barely recognize—someone who's tasted the kind of power that comes not from force, but from the sweetest surrender.

"Clearly." Vlad's knowing gaze finds mine, carrying weight beyond mere words. "Though some of us seem intent on changing *everything* at once."

The bourbon burns less than the truth in his observation. Around us, the study holds its breath—centuries of Ursa secrets pressed into ancient wood and leather, bearing witness to yet another turning point in our clan's history.

Outside, snow continues to fall, each flake a choice made, a future altered.

"You're one to talk about change," Samara retorts, her eyes glinting like obsidian. "The lone wolf who swore no omega would ever touch his heart."

"And gave you a niece whose power already rivals ancient bloodlines," Vlad counters, helping himself to more bourbon. His silver eyes carry that peculiar softness they get when speaking of his mate and cub—Anya's rare omega magic having proven as potent as any alpha's.

"How is little Katya, by the way?" Samara asks,

tension easing from her shoulders as we step onto safer ground. "Missing her favorite aunt, I'm sure."

"Her *only* aunt," I remind her, but my voice lacks its usual edge. The mention of Vlad's daughter softens something in my chest. "How is she?"

"Growing too fast." Pride and longing war in his voice, making the air thick with emotion. "Already showing signs of shifting. Her eyes went silver yesterday."

"So young..." Samara breathes, wonder replacing her earlier defiance. "She'll be powerful."

"Like her mother." Vlad's smile turns wistful, remembering his fierce mate who defied every prediction about her supposedly weaker bloodline. "Speaking of powerful mates..." His knowing gaze shifts to Samara. "A dragon, сестренка? Really?"

"About Nikolaas..." I shift my attention to my sister. The study reminds me of home tonight—dark wood panels holding centuries of secrets, snow falling beyond leaded glass, the quiet conspiracy of family sharing drinks and deeper truths. "Have you considered what becoming his mate will mean when the time comes?"

Samara's hand flies to her throat, where in six months' time the dragon's bite will mark her as his. The gesture makes her look younger still, vulnerable in a way that stirs my protective instincts. "Of course I have."

"Being mate to the most powerful shifter in the world is no small thing, Sam." The hearth's flames paint her face in amber light. Time has barely touched her, while Vlad and I carry shadows in our eyes. "When the claiming ritual takes place, you'll have influence beyond anything you can fathom."

"You think I chose him for power?" A dangerous edge creeps into her voice, sharp as Siberian wind.

"No." I move to the drink cart. The familiar ritual of pouring drinks steadies me—three measures of bourbon, because even in this, we remain a trinity. "I think you chose him because he sets your blood on fire and makes you forget yourself." A wry smirk tugs at my lips.

Vlad's soft chuckle carries understanding beyond words as I hand them each a glass. Samara's eyes widen at the gesture—she knows how rarely I permit her indulgence. But tonight feels like home, like those endless Russian nights when we three would huddle in Father's study, sharing secrets and spinning dreams.

"The power that comes with being his mate is simply... convenient," I add, watching amber liquid catch light like captured sunsets.

She takes the drink, her hand trembling slightly.

Behind her, Vlad settles deeper into his leather chair, silver eyes gleaming, a wolf guarding his pack. "And the months of waiting? Are they *convenient* too?"

"Traditional." I lean against the mantle. The crystal in my hand glints against the flickering flames, transforming bourbon into liquid amber, into memories of winters past when our greatest worry was Father catching us sharing his best spirits. "Our clan understands the importance of waiting."

"And yet you branded Cassandra within *days* of meeting her," she counters, voice soft as new snow. Her fingers trace the rim of her glass, creating notes that shiver through the air like half-formed spells.

The bourbon turns to ice in my throat. In his corner of the study, Vlad goes preternaturally still, that absolute stillness only predators achieve when scenting approaching storms.

"Our alliance couldn't wait." The admission scrapes across my tongue like shattered ice. "But you and Nikolaas—you have the luxury of doing this properly. Of letting your magic ripen naturally before it meets dragon fire."

"And what if I don't want to wait?" Samara's words cut through the study's warmth, sharp with that particular brand of recklessness that comes only with youth and untested power. "What if my magic is ready now? What if—"

"Достаточно." *That's enough.* Vlad cuts her off, his voice rough with affection even as he plucks the glass from her fingers. Despite his stern expression, love softens the edges of his command—the same way it always has, since she was small enough to ride on his shoulders through snowy Saint Petersburg streets. "No more booze for you, **мой маленький**."

Samara scowls, but something softens in her expression at his use of the childhood endearment. Even at twenty, fierce as she pretends to be, she's still the little sister who used to beg him for one more story about wolf packs running under winter moons. She settles deeper into her chair, that particular mix of defiance and grace that marks her as truly Alexeev.

"Your magic may be ready," he continues, swirling the bourbon in his glass, "but are *you*? Magic without control is destruction waiting to happen. You've seen it before, Sam. We all have."

Samara's defiance wavers, her lips parting as though to argue, but the weight of Vlad's words settles over her like snowfall, heavy and undeniable. For a moment, the only sound in the study is the crackle of the fire and the faint howl of the wind beyond the frosted windows.

"I'm not a child anymore," she says softly, her voice stripped of its earlier sharpness. "I know what I'm doing."

"Do you?" I ask, stepping closer. My tone is gentler now, but no less firm. "Don't let impatience blind you to what's at stake."

Her dark eyes meet mine, a flicker of doubt shadowing her determination. "And what about you, brother? You lecture me about patience, yet you bound Cassandra without giving her the same choice."

The accusation strikes true, the unspoken truth in her words twisting in my chest. "I did what I had to," I say after a moment, my voice as steady as the ground beneath us. "To protect her, to protect us all. It wasn't a choice—it was my duty."

"Duty," Samara echoes bitterly, turning back to the fire. "Always the burden of duty."

Vlad sets his glass down with a deliberate clink, breaking the tense silence. "We're all bound by something," he says, his voice softer now. "By duty, by loyalty, by love. The question isn't what binds us—it's what we *choose* to do with those bonds."

Samara's shoulders relax slightly, her tension melting into the warmth of the fire. "You sound just like Father," she says, a faint smile tugging at her lips.

Vlad chuckles, the sound rich and warm despite the chill lingering in the room. "I have my moments of wisdom."

I allow the stillness to permeate the air, the comforting warmth of the fire bridging the gap between us. For all our differences, we're still a family—bound together by blood, by magic, by the shared oaths to our supernatural world.

"We have pressing matters to discuss," I say, my voice rough with countless emotions. I move to my desk, withdrawing Nikolaas' invitation from the top drawer. "The Yule dinner."

"Mm," Vlad utters, clearly relieved for the change in subject. "The dragon's grand debut as alpha."

Samara's eyes brighten at the mention, though she tries to hide it behind her usual sharp wit. "Should be interesting, watching him juggle all those egos in one room."

"*More* than interesting." I spread the invitation on the desk, its heavy cream paper somehow ominous in the room's twilight. "Every major supernatural player will be there, watching. Waiting."

"For what exactly?" Vlad asks, though his smug tone implies he already knows.

"For their shot at the game." I trace the dragon seal with my finger. "The slightest flaw will do. In

Nikolaas' leadership, in our alliance with the Deverauxs, in..." I pause, meeting Samara's gaze. "In all of us."

My sister straightens under my scrutiny. "I know where my loyalties lie, brother," she all but hisses, wounded by my insinuation.

"Are you certain?" The words emerge softly, yet no less lethal. "Because tonight, more than ever, you need to remember who you are." I move around the desk to stand before her. "You are not *his*. You're Samara Alexeeva. Ursa Princess. Remember that."

A flash of defiance ignites in her dark eyes. "I can be both."

"No," I say firmly. "Not yet. Not until the claiming. For now, you are of *our* blood, *our* clan. The Drakens..." I glance at the invitation again. "They may be allies, but they are not family. Not for six more months."

"The Drakens are not to be trusted," Vlad joins in, holding Samara's rebellious stare. "Not completely. Never completely."

"Like the Deverauxs?" she challenges, nails digging into the leather armchair.

"The Deverauxs are different."

"Because you've branded one of them?" The words slip like venom from her tongue. "Tell me, brother, how is magically forcing loyalty any different from falling in love with it?"

"Sam..." Vlad warns, but she's already ignited my temper.

"You think this is about love?" I slam my hand on the desk, making the bourbon glasses rattle. "This is about endurance. About keeping our clan strong when every other supernatural family waits, desperate to see our downfall." I pause, reining in my anger. "What do you think would happen if the Ursa Princess appeared too eager to submit to dragon rule?"

"Submit?" She practically spits the word. "Is that what you think—"

"It's what *they'll* think," I cut her off. "The other clans, the covens, every creature of power who'll be watching tonight. They'll see the Alexeev princess falling at a dragon's feet, and they'll smell blood in the water."

Samara's face pales, but her chin lifts higher. "I don't fall at anyone's feet."

"Then prove it." I soften my tone, reaching for her hand. "Show them the pride of the Ursa clan runs deeper than any romantic attachment. Show them that even in love, an Alexeev bows to no one."

"Not even to the future king of dragons?" Her voice carries a hint of humor now.

"*Especially* not to him." I squeeze her fingers. "Let him earn you, сестренка. Make him prove he's worthy of Ursa blood."

"Besides," Vlad interjects with a sly grin, "what fun is the chase if you make it too easy for him?"

Samara rolls her eyes, but the tension in her shoulders eases. "You would know all about that, wouldn't you? How long did Anya make *you* wait?"

"That's not fair," he says, though his smile turns wistful. "She was on her own then. Innocent to our ways."

"And now?" I ask, genuinely curious about my brother's mate.

"Now she's the strongest wolf I've ever known." Pride colors his voice. "And the best mother our daughter could have."

The mention of Katya shifts something in the room's atmosphere. Family. The one we've lost, the one we're building, the ones we choose and the ones who choose us.

"Speaking of strong women," Samara says, moving to the window where snow continues to fall, "what do you plan to do about Cassandra's growing power?"

I join her at the window, watching as the grounds of our ancestral home disappear under fresh white. "What I must," I say finally. "What I've always done. Protect our clan, maintain our alliances, and…" I pause, remembering violet flames in stormy eyes. "And hope I haven't completely misjudged the situation."

"When do you ever misjudge anything?" Vlad asks, but there's no mockery in his tone.

Thoughts of Luciana and Sestroretsk flood my mind, along with the weight of decisions fueled by grief and rage. "More often than you'd believe, brother." I pivot away from the window. "We must prepare ourselves. Tonight's dinner will be a test for us all."

My siblings depart, leaving me alone in my study. Outside, the snow falls silently, covering up any trace of the day's activities. Somewhere in Paris, Cassandra readies herself for the night ahead, her magic probably making the very air around her sizzle with power.

As darkness descends, so does our fate. The price we must pay may be too steep for us to bear. But whatever comes our way, I'll be ready.

6

NIK

My dragon magic bleeds into every corner of Draken Manor, coating windows in ice crystals that have nothing to do with winter chill. I've made sure of that, letting my power seep into the stone, the wood, the very air they'll breathe. Let them feel it the moment they cross my threshold—this is still dragon territory, half clan or not.

Bram's betrayal echoes in the empty eastern wing. My brother took more than just his loyalists when he left; he tore away half our ancestral wards, protections woven through centuries. But a dragon adapts.

I trace patterns in the frost, dragon fire shimmering beneath ice—my new wards, my own touch on this Yule gathering. The manor appears cavernous now, too hollow without the clan's full might. Perhaps that's fitting. A dragon needs room to spread his wings, after all.

A commotion in the foyer pulls at my senses. Too early for guests, which means—

"Sir." My steward arrives, slightly breathless. Even his usual composure can't quite mask his unease. "The Ursa King's men are here to inspect the premises."

Of course. His sister's mate or not, Gavriil would sooner tear out his own heart than risk Samara. The thought brings an involuntary smile to my lips, yet it fades as I remember our precarious position.

"Let them do their job," I say, though my beast snarls at the thought of other predators marking our territory. "But make sure they understand—this is still Draken land."

Even if my own blood no longer recognizes it as such.

Bear magic leaves a musty trail through my halls as Gavriil's guards move with calculated precision. The scent makes my inner dragon restless, territorial instincts warring with political necessity. Sasha leads them—more shadow than shifter, Gavriil's most lethal weapon wrapped in a courtier's manners. His cold eyes miss nothing. I can sense him testing every corner, every shadow, searching for weakenesses in my defenses.

"The wards are impressive," he says in that low, accented voice that gives nothing away. "But they've been recently changed."

My jaw clenches. "The old ones went with my brother." The words cling to my tongue like poison. Centuries of carefully maintained protections, gone in a single night of betrayal. "These are of my making."

Interest sharpens Sasha's gaze. Most know dragons for our fire, our fury—not the intricate magic of wards. That's witch territory. But necessity breeds invention, and I've had to become more than what they expect.

"The Ursa King will want to add his own protections for the evening." Not a request. Never a request from Gavriil's people.

"Of course." I force my voice to stay neutral, though my dragon rages at the thought of foreign magic coated over mine. "As long as he understands my wards remain primary."

A test, wrapped in courtesy. Will the mighty Ursa King respect my authority in my own den? Sasha's slight nod tells me he reads every layer of meaning.

"There is also the matter of..." A careful pause, political as a blade. "Seating arrangements."

Ah. Now we come to it.

"The Ursa King and his chosen mate must be positioned appropriately." Sasha's remarks cut straight to the wound. "Given recent... developments with your clan."

My brother's empty chair. The glaring reminder of our fractured strength that every supernatural creature will notice later tonight. Gavriil wants to ensure his sister isn't seated anywhere that might diminish her status—or worse, suggest the Alexeevs support the wrong side of this family feud. As if Samara would ever...

The thought breaks as her scent hits me—winter roses and cool lightning cutting through the musty traces of bear magic. My pulse quickens before I can control it.

She appears in the doorway like midnight made flesh, her dark eyes sparkling with that mischief that makes my dragon stir. "Sorry to interrupt," she says, though her smile tells me she's anything *but* sorry. "I need to borrow the dragon for a moment."

Tension ripples through Sasha's shoulders. His fundamental duty is protecting the Ursa Princess, and here she is, strolling into what he considers enemy territory. The irony would be amusing if it didn't make my blood burn.

"My lady," Sasha starts, "the premises haven't been fully secured—"

"Then consider this a test of your security measures," she counters as she moves into the room with that ferocious grace that reminds me she's as much warrior as princess. "Besides, what safer place could I be than with a dragon in his own lair?"

The double meaning in her words sends heat coursing through my veins. "Leave us," I order, unable to take my eyes off her. "We'll finish the inspection later."

I catch Sasha's hesitation, the way his gaze flicks between us before he bows. "As you wish." Ever the perfect soldier, even when his instincts must be screaming to protect his charge. He ushers the other guards out, closing the doors behind them.

The moment we're alone, the careful mask of Ursa Princess falls from her exquisite features. "I missed you," she breathes, and my beast roars in response to the vulnerability in her voice.

"It's been sixteen hours and forty-three minutes," I say, my tone low. "But who's counting?" I'm already reaching for her, drinking in her scent, the way her power hums against mine.

"Hours of my brother lecturing me about proper behavior around dragons." Her fingers trace my jaw, each touch like sparks against my skin. "About maintaining Ursa pride and not appearing too... eager."

"And are you?" I catch her wandering hand, pressing my lips to her palm where her pulse races. "Eager?"

"Always." The way her eyes darken makes me want to forget every rule, every tradition keeping us apart. "But don't let it go to your head. Dragons are already insufferably arrogant."

"Says the Ursa princess who once called us overgrown lizards." I lean down, letting my breath ghost across her ear. My dragon preens at the way she shivers. "Your brother would be scandalized if he could see you now."

"My brother," she says with that wicked smile that haunts my dreams, "isn't here."

"No." My hands find her waist, pulling her closer. "He isn't."

Her breath catches as our bodies meet. My dragon stirs, responding to her nearness, to the way her magic crackles against mine like storm meeting flame. Six months. Six endless months until I can claim her properly. The thought is exquisite torture.

"The manor looks beautiful," she whispers, but her eyes remain fixed on my mouth. "All this frost... it's not traditional dragon decor, is it?"

"I'm not a traditional dragon." I trace the curve of her spine, savoring her shiver. So much power in such a delicate frame. "Does that bother you?"

"Nothing about you bothers me." She rises on her toes, her lips a breath away from mine. "Except maybe how long you're taking to kiss me."

A laugh rumbles through my chest, dragon-deep. "So impatient, little bear."

The corner of her mouth curls in a sensual smile. "Six months is a long time to be patient."

The reminder of our waiting period sends fresh heat through my blood. I catch her chin between my fingers, tilting her face up. Her pulse races under my touch. "Worth every second," I growl, before claiming her mouth.

She tastes of winter wind and wild honey, her lips soft but demanding. My power surges in response, making the ice crystals on the windows pulse with blue fire. Her hands slip into my hair, pulling me closer, and my control frays at the edges. When she opens to me, deepening the kiss, it takes every ounce of restraint not to claim her here and now.

When we break apart, our chests heaving with excitement, her eyes have shifted to bear-gold. The sight makes my dragon roar with pride—I did that, pulled her far enough from control to have her Ursa power show through.

"Gavriil will smell you all over me," she murmurs against my lips.

"Good." The word emerges more growl than speech. Let her brother remember who she's chosen. Who she belongs to, politics be damned.

Her fingers trace patterns over my heart, each touch stoking the fire in my blood. The dragon under my skin writhes, demanding more. Sam's power meets mine like ice kissing flame, and for a moment I see what we'll become—alpha pair, dragon and bear united, forging a path no one has dared before.

"Tonight will change everything," she whispers, echoing my thoughts. "The other clans will be watching..."

"Let them watch." I cup her face between my hands, memorizing every detail—the flush staining her cheeks, how her pupils dilate when my thumb traces her lower lip. My territory, my mate, my future. "Let them see exactly what we are."

"And what are we?" Her question carries weight beyond this moment, beyond stolen kisses and secret meetings. Her strength thrums against mine, bear and dragon dancing on the knife's edge of inevitability.

My power responds before I can answer, frost

crackling across windows with renewed intensity. Her stare tracks the patterns, wonder blooming in her dark eyes as my magic paints the room in crystalline light. Her fingers press against my thundering heart, and for an instant, I forget about politics, about waiting periods, about everything except her.

"We're the future," I tell her, savoring prophecy in the words. "All that is happening now—Bram's departure, your brother's alliance with the Deverauxs, this gathering tonight—it's all part of something bigger."

"Something terrifying," she adds with that smile that makes my dragon want to burn the world.

"Something magnificent." I lean down, pressing my forehead to hers. "Like you."

Her laugh curls through me, soft and threaded with desire. "Now who's being impatient?"

"Six months," I remind us both, though the words emerge as more growl than speech. My dragon claws at my control, demanding to claim her now, tradition be damned. "Six months until I can show the world exactly what you mean to me."

"And tonight?" Her fingers slip down to my nape, drawing me in, and my restraint threatens to snap.

"Tonight," I purr, "we give them a preview."

When I take her mouth again, it's with all the heat of dragon fire. She meets me with equal hunger, and for these precious moments, everything else burns away—politics, clan loyalties, the weight of centuries of tradition. There is only this: the taste of her lips, the press of her body against mine, our magic dancing together like lovers' hands.

Where we touch, power sparks across skin. Dragon flame meeting bear strength. Fire and ice, ancient magics colliding in ways that make the very air shimmer. The frost patterns on my windows pulse with our shared heartbeat, casting ethereal shadows that paint us in winter twilight.

Samara pulls back first, her breathing uneven. "We shouldn't," she whispers, but her fingers still clutch my shirt like she can't bear to let go. "The staff will talk."

"Let them." My voice emerges rough with barely contained power. Six months of waiting suddenly seems like an eternal torment with her, warm and willing, in my arms.

A tendril of her dark chestnut hair escapes its careful styling, and I brush it back, letting my fingers linger on the soft skin where my claiming mark will eventually rest. Her pulse jumps beneath my caress, making my dragon purr.

"You're making this very difficult," she says,

though the smile in her voice soothes my dragon's pride.

"Good." The word rumbles from deep in my chest. "Difficulty builds character."

"Oh, is that it?" Her eyes dance with mischief that makes me want to discard every obligation, every duty. "I thought you were just trying to drive me mad before the six months are up."

"That too." I trace the slope of her neck, reveling at how she leans into my touch. Even this small surrender feeds my dragon's possessive nature. "Though your brother might kill me first."

"Gavriil has his own problems." Something flickers in her expression—concern bleeding through desire. "Have you noticed anything... strange about Cassandra lately?"

The question pulls me back to reality like ice water in my veins. Politics and power plays await us beyond these doors. Tonight isn't just about showcasing new alliances—it's about maintaining the delicate balance that keeps our world hidden from mortal eyes.

"Strange how?" I ask, though I've sensed it too—the way magic seems to bend around the Deveraux witch, like reality itself responds to her presence. It sets my dragon's teeth on edge.

"I don't know," she admits. "But I think we should keep an eye on her."

"We will." My hands slide to her hips. There will be time for strategy later. Right now, my dragon demands only one thing—her warmth against me.

Her lips part under my touch, beckoning me in for more. Our tongues dance slowly at first, then more urgently as our need grows. She tastes like sweet wine and dark chocolate with a hint of cinnamon that sends my senses reeling. Her body melts into mine, fitting perfectly against my hard length. My hands explore the soft expanse of her back, tracing the lines of her spine before sliding downward to cup her perfect behind.

Moans escape us as I press her closer, welcoming the heat between us as it grows. The scent of her arousal mingles with the sweet smoke from the nearby hearth, filling the air with an intoxicating perfume that makes me dizzy with desire.

I dip my head lower, nipping at the column of her throat before trailing kisses along the valley between her breasts. She arches into me, gasping softly as I roll one of her tight nipples between my fingers. It hardens beneath my touch, and she moans quietly against my mouth.

"It's been too long," I murmur against her skin. "Too damn long."

She nods in agreement, pressing herself closer still. My desire for her grows into an ache that threatens to consume me whole. With a low growl, I pick her up effortlessly and carry her toward my desk —our own personal dais transformed by twilight into a bed of risqué endeavors.

Knowing she likes it rough, I tear off her dress swiftly, revealing toned legs and rounded hips encased in sheer black lace panties that match the bra currently pushed up around her ribcage. Her maroon eyes watch me hungrily as I toss aside my suit jacket before unfastening my pants and letting them drop to the floor without ceremony. My manhood springs free, already hard and aching for release.

She gasps at the sight of it—thick and veined with anticipation—before stepping out of her ruined panties and bra to stand naked before me at last. We're both flushed with need by this point; every muscle tensed, hungry for what comes next.

Wasting no time, I lift her up onto the desk so she straddles me waist-deep while pressing herself against my rigid length. Electricity hisses between us as we grind together, slowly at first, then faster until there's no doubt where this is going.

"Do you want me inside you?" I ask, my voice ragged with lust. She bites her bottom lip in response —an unspoken *yes* that sends shivers down my spine. "Yeah? How badly do you want it?"

A nod, this time accompanied by a moan as she slides her hands down my chest to grip my hips firmly. "*Please!*" she gasps.

She moans loudly as I finally push through the fabric barrier between us and enter her slick heat in one powerful stroke that fills both our minds with white lightning flashes of pleasure-pain unlike anything else imaginable. Our bodies move together instinctively now—hers riding mine like a wild thing, driven by some ancient primal instinct while I bite and suck at her neck, tasting her sweat mixed with desire on my tongue.

The air fills with the sound of ripping silk as it gives way beneath us, revealing my bare chest to her touch and allowing her more leverage for grinding against me. The taste of victory—and something else —lingers on her lips when she finally pulls away to look into my eyes. "More," she whispers hoarsely. "Nik, please!"

I oblige by sliding one hand under her rear end to lift her higher onto me while the other grips fistfuls of her hair, urging her head back towards mine. Our mouths crash together in a desperate kiss that tastes like forbidden fruit and sweat-soaked skin as we pound against each other without mercy or restraint. I can feel her walls clenching tight around me, signaling her approach to climax with every powerful thrust up into her body.

"Come for me, Sam," I growl against her lips, my release drawing near as well. "Let go for me!"

And then it hits us both. An explosion of ecstasy so intense it seems to shake the very foundations of reality itself. Together, we cry out each other's names in unison as our bodies tremor uncontrollably from the force of this primal union. Sweat drips from our foreheads onto the now-torn remains of my shirt as we ride out our mutual orgasms, my seed filling her up while she milks every last drop of pleasure from me with greedy moans and gasps that echo through the otherwise silent room.

Finally spent, we collapse onto the ruins of my office, panting heavily as if we've just run a marathon uphill. The scent of sex fills the air around us like a heavy perfume, mingling with the taste of triumph and loss on our lips and tongues alike.

"That was… quite a preview," she whispers, sweet exhaustion threaded in her voice.

I glide my fingers along the curve of her jaw,

committing to memory the way twilight dances across her flushed skin. If she only knew what dragon magic could do when wholly unleashed, how claiming marks seared deeper than mere flesh. These stolen moments, these careful tastes of what we could be—they're nothing compared to what will ignite between us when her powers fully awaken, when she comes of age and my fire can finally claim her completely.

"My little bear," I murmur against her temple, and she shivers at the promise in my voice, "you have no idea what awaits you." Dragon magic stirs beneath my skin, responding to the thought of future claims, of powers merging in ways that could reshape worlds. "Six months will feel like eternity, but when they're over..." I let the words trail off, secretly satisfied as her pulse quickens.

As I look down at her flushed cheeks and heaving chest, all I can think is: *My love. My mate... This is what it feels like to be truly alive.*

7

CASSANDRA

A spark of magic ignites within me as I gaze at Draken Manor. Imposing, the ancestral home looms against the twilight sky, its windows gleaming with enchanted frost—Nikolaas' power made manifest. Even from a distance, I can sense his dragon magic rippling through the air, testing the boundaries of my own untamed power.

"Ready, printsessa?" Gavriil's voice carries that damned edge of dominance that makes his brand pulse within me. His firm hand settles at the small of my back, possessive and protective all at once.

I want to say *no*. Want to run from this gathering of supernatural creatures who will surely sense the chaos brewing inside me. But the crimson silk of my gown whispers against my skin, reminding me of Ivan's words: *Make them question everything.*

"As I'll ever be," I manage, grateful that the falling snow masks the tremor in my voice.

We ascend the manor's steps, and I recognize the moment we cross the threshold of Nikolaas' wards. Dragon magic wraps around us like invisible wings, testing, measuring. For a heart-stopping moment, it tangles with the tempestuous force growing inside me, and I fear everything will shatter.

But then Gavriil's hand tightens on my waist, his brand flaring to life, and somehow the confluence of magic stabilizes. His sudden stillness speaks volumes —pupils contracting to deadly points as his power perceives mine.

"Fascinating," he murmurs, but before I can ask what he means, the doors swing open.

The grand ballroom unfolds before us like a winter fairytale gone dark. Crystal chandeliers cast prismatic light across enchanted frost, each surface gleaming with dragon fire trapped beneath ice. The assembled supernatural elite stand in careful clusters, power radiating from them in waves that make the very air shimmer.

Near the eastern windows, the Rousseau clan commands attention without seeking it—Adrien and

Henri, alpha pair of the Lyon wolf packs. Their matching black suits emphasize rather than diminish their wild nature, pitch-black hair and silver eyes scanning the crowd with predatory grace while their fingers remain intertwined. Even here, among the most powerful of our kind, few dare approach the mated pair directly. Their love story has transcended into legend. Two alphas finding strength in submission to each other rather than dominance over a pack.

The Nordic Wolves cluster near the grand fireplace, their alpha radiating that particular brand of ancient power that comes from bloodlines older than written history. Einar Wolfhart's silver hair catches firelight like fresh snow, his quiet authority belying his beast's volatile nature.

Gavriil guides me through the crowd with practiced ease, his presence both anchor and cage. Each step feels like walking on knives as my magic writhes within my core, responding to the press of so many supernatural energies. Vampire, witch, warlock, shifter—their combined power creates a symphony that threatens to overwhelm my senses.

"Breathe," Gavriil murmurs, his lips barely moving. His thumb traces lazy circles on my lower back, and damn him, but the touch helps ground me.

The brand recognizes its maker, even as the wild magic inside me rebels against its constraints.

We pause before Nikolaas, who stands resplendent in midnight blue that makes his ocean eyes gleam like ancient treasure. Dragon magic rolls off him with ease, transforming the surrounding air into something sharp and electric. When his gaze meets mine, I know he's testing the edges of my power, curious and wary all at once.

"Welcome to Draken Manor," he says, but his eyes drift to something beyond my shoulder. Something softens in his expression, and I know without looking that Samara has entered.

The temperature in the room shifts subtly as she approaches. Bear magic meets dragon fire. It's then that I glimpse what they might become. An alliance of age-old forces, capable of reshaping our reality. Yet as my powers surge in response, I must grit my teeth until the metallic tang of blood fills my mouth to keep them in check.

"The Ursa King and his chosen mate honor us," Nikolaas continues, though the words sound hollow, mere ceremony masking deeper currents. Political theatre for the watching crowd.

"The honor is ours," Gavriil replies smoothly, but

his fingers press harder against my spine. He feels it too—the way the gathered forces swirl and eddy around us, testing boundaries, seeking frailties.

Somewhere in the crowd, I catch a flash of familiar green eyes. A vampire in a den of shifters—unheard of until now, when the Deveraux Grand Witch has risen from the grave. Ivan watches from the shadows, champagne glass in hand, his presence a silent promise of protection. But even he can't shield me from what's coming.

The child inside me stirs, and with it, power older than time itself.

Magic ripples through the ballroom like dark water, each supernatural creature adding their own current to the dangerous tide. The rebellious strength rising inside me responds to every shift, every eddy, making the crystal chandeliers tremble ever so slightly. No one else seems to notice, too caught up in their careful waltz of power and politics.

"Shall we?" Gavriil's voice sails through with that edge of velvet-laced steel that sets my nerves on fire. His hand slides to my waist as the first strains of music fill the air—something classical and haunting that makes my magic pulse in time with the violins.

I have no choice but to step into his embrace,

letting him guide me onto the dance floor. His brand sings beneath my skin, countering the torrent raging in my blood. His hand settles on my lower back, and his sharp intake of breath tells me he senses the raw power pulsing beneath his touch.

"You're stronger tonight," he murmurs, turning us in a graceful sweep that makes my crimson skirts flare. "The air practically bends around you."

I can't help but wonder if he has finally caught on to the truth. Has he unraveled the mystery and seen it for what it truly is? The secret burns in my throat, makes my magic surge dangerously close to the surface. I refuse to give the Ursa King another reason to despise my child, another weapon for him to use against the innocent life I carry.

My gaze shifts away, and I notice a champagne glass fracturing into delicate shards, yet no one seems to pay it any mind.

"Perhaps it's the company we keep," I manage, nodding subtly toward where Nikolaas and Samara dance, dragon and bear magic twining around them like visible auras. Their power should overwhelm everything else in the room, and still...

"No." Gavriil's grip hardens against my spine, controlling and questioning all at once. "This is something else. Something older. And it definitely has *no ties* to my brand."

The music swells, and with it, my carefully maintained control begins to slip. Power radiates through me, and I sense the exact moment Gavriil's branding spell struggles to contain the magic surging within me.

His eyes narrow, spectral blue flames igniting in their depths. "What aren't you telling me, printsessa?" he all but hisses.

The question hangs between us like frost before a storm, but I can't answer—not here, not with dozens of supernatural creatures watching our every move. Instead, I let Gavriil guide me through another turn, buying precious seconds as I struggle to suppress the magic threatening to break free.

The chandeliers above us chime softly, crystals singing in response to the power building beneath my skin. Each note reverberates through my bones, through the life growing inside me, until I can barely distinguish where my magic ends and the child's begins. Dristan's child—the thought alone makes the violet flames in my eyes burn brighter.

Gavriil's grip tightens, his brand igniting as it tries to restrain whatever is happening. But for the first time, his magic falters, uncertainty bleeding through his usual iron control. His eyes search mine, and beneath the predatory gleam, I glimpse something else—not fear exactly, but a dawning realization that makes my heart stutter.

"The magic..." he whispers, his voice rough with discovery. "It's not just *yours* anymore, is it?"

The words strike like lightning. Around us, the enchanted frost on the windows begins to crack, hairline fractures spreading in delicate patterns that mirror my rising panic. Behind Gavriil, Nikolaas starts, aware of the disturbance. His dragon magic subtly swells in response, trying to maintain control of his territory, but even his formidable power seems distant compared to the maelstrom building inside me.

"Oh, gods..." I breathe. "Not now."

A champagne glass shatters somewhere to our left. The music wavers, strings going discordant as my power affects our surroundings. And through it all, Gavriil's dark eyes bore into mine, seeing too much, understanding too much.

His touch slips to my still-flat stomach, and the brand pulses once, violently. "Impossible," he breathes, but we both know that's a lie. In our world, *impossible* is merely a challenge waiting to be overcome.

A ripple of dark power expands through my being, electrifying and dreary as it fills me with a heavy sense of foreboding.

Time crystallizes around us, each second sharp as shattered glass. The weight of Gavriil's hand against my stomach feels like a brand of its own, his magic probing at the impossible truth growing within me. Above us, the chandeliers' light fragments into prismatic shards, casting otherworldly shadows across his face as understanding blooms in his dark eyes.

"The vampire's child?" he breathes, the words barely audible above the discordant music. "*He's* the source of this power?" His grip stiffens, his bear magic encountering something primal and untamed—energy that makes even the mighty Ursa King take half a step back.

The room spins around us, a dizzying waltz of supernatural energies colliding. Dragon fire, bear strength, witch magic, and something completely different collide. Through the chaos, I catch glimpses of the others: Ivan's face draining of color as he realizes what's happening, Juliette's amethyst eyes widening with recognition, Samara frozen mid-dance in Nikolaas' arms.

"The brand," Gavriil growls, his tone something between wonder and fury. "It wasn't just fighting your magic. It was trying to protect..." He can't finish the sentence, but his hand remains splayed across my abdomen, caught between possessive and protective.

Violet flames flicker at the edges of my vision, threatening to consume me. I know then my frail control has finally crumbled. The windows rattle in their frames. The enchanted frost cracks like breaking ice. Even the air seems to bend and twist around us, reality warping under the pressure of this overwhelming power.

"Gavriil," I manage, my voice breaking on his name. "I can't—"

The words shatter into amethyst beams as my magic explodes outward. Windows burst, sending shards of glass spinning through frost-laden air. But something else breaks too—not just glass and ice, but time itself. Reality ripples like disturbed water, the walls of Draken Manor becoming transparent as smoke.

Through my hazed vision, I glimpse Juliette across the room, her form shimmering, fading, as if being pulled into some other moment. The mistletoe carvings in the doorframes pulse with ancient light, responding to this fracture in time. Gasps rise from the unsettled crowd, couples scattering on the dance floor, their movement slow as shadows stretching under a dying sun.

The last thing I see before darkness claims me is my grandmother's face. Juliette, draped in taffeta and lace. Suddenly, she's young and full of hope, unaware of the centuries of choices stretching before her.

8

JULIETTE

Reality tears like black velvet around me, and I fall through time itself. When the world snaps back into place, I'm standing in Deveraux Manor's grand dining room, but not my manor—not the one where I now live. This is the manor of my youth, still innocent of the tragedies to come that will shape the next three hundred years.

The Yule dinner has just ended. Pine boughs drape over every surface, their sharp winter scent mingling with spiced wine and memories so powerful they make my chest ache. Candlelight paints everything in shades of honey and gold, exactly as I remember it. Exactly as it was before everything changed.

My hands tremble as I smooth them over my gown—not the rose gold silk I wore instants ago, but the cream-colored taffeta and lace of my seventeenth year. My body feels different too, younger, unburdened by centuries of choices and regrets.

And then I see him.

Willem stands by the hearth, golden hair catching firelight like captured sunrise. He's so young, so beautiful it hurts to look at him. No shadows haunt his eyes yet, no hint of the darkness that would eventually consume us both. When he turns, his smile is pure and true—the smile of a man who still believes in love.

"There you are," he says, and his voice—gods above and below, his voice without the weight of time —makes something in my chest crack open. "I was beginning to think you'd escaped through some secret passage."

I should fight this. Should try to tear my way back through time to Ivan and the life I've reclaimed. But my body remembers this dance even as my mind rebels against it. This moment feels like drowning in honey—sweet and suffocating all at once.

"The dinner went well," I hear myself say, though the words taste strangely on my tongue. How young I sound, how innocent of the fate that looms ahead.

"It did." Willem moves closer, and the air around us grows thick with dragon magic—clean and sharp, nothing like the corrupted power he'll later wield.

The light catches something above us—last winter's mistletoe, preserved by magic, still hanging from the dark beams. Willem follows my gaze and reaches up, fingers brushing one pearly berry. A jolt goes through me—not his touch this time, but true Sight. For a heartbeat, I glimpse what fate has preordained: a child with violet flames dancing in their eyes, ancient plants blooming fresh and green in deepest winter… The vision fades before I can grasp its meaning.

"Just now, you saw something," Willem murmurs, his presence filling my senses the way it did back then, before I knew what real darkness tasted like.

His fingers brush my cheek, and I shiver—not from fear or revulsion as I should, but from the ghost of feelings I thought long buried. This Willem hasn't learned cruelty yet. This Willem's touch still carries warmth instead of frost.

"I was thinking about… the claiming," I whisper, knowing my role in this old conversation. Part of me wants to scream warnings to my younger self, to tell her what that brand will eventually cost us all. But the words stick in my throat like honey-coated thorns.

"Three years," he purrs, inching close enough to scent my neck, quietly yearning to cast his dragon's bite. "I don't think I can wait that long."

And you won't, I answer inwardly.

His thumb traces my lower lip, and dragon fire sparks between us, pure and intoxicating. My magic responds instinctively, an amethyst gleam pulsing from me as our powers entwine. "Endless months until I can mark you as mine, until everyone knows you belong to me."

I remember this moment—how those words once made my heart soar with possibility rather than dread. How could I have known then that possession would turn to obsession? That love would twist into something darker than shadow?

"We should say goodnight to your grandmother," he says, offering his arm with that courtly grace that once made me believe in fairy tales. "Though I confess, I'm tempted to steal you away instead."

"Take what you want, my dragon lord," I taunt back as I bow my head, knowing full well the arc of this story.

A smug smile curls his lips, his dragon's pride satisfied by my submission. "Break the rules?" he asks, his hands gliding on my waist, pulling me closer.

"We shall make new ones." My heart thrums

violently against my ribs as I inch closer towards him until there's nothing between us but air—and then his warmth. He exhales heavily against my mouth before pressing his lips gently against mine, tasting like mint and power and longing. Time seems to stand still as we lose ourselves in each other's embrace under this starlit canopy.

Our tongues tangle together like kindred spirits finding home after years of wandering aimlessly through life's maze. His hands wander lower, exploring every dip and curve of my body as if mapping out uncharted terrain. Teeth nip at my bottom lip, making me gasp softly. His fingers trace patterns along my inner thigh, causing goosebumps to rise despite the heat building between us.

We break apart for air—gasping heavily—only for his lips to find their way back to mine again. Harder this time, demanding more from me than just mere pleasure.

"Sweet gods, Juliette," he purrs, soft lips grazing the slope of my neck. His hips grind against mine rhythmically as if seeking something primal that neither of us can name yet alone deny at this point. "I would burn the world for you and lay it at your feet. Surely, you must know this."

My breath comes out in a shaky whisper as I gaze

at Willem, "Now, I do." My cheeks flush with youthful impulsiveness and burning desire. Until now, I had foolishly believed that he saw me as an equal, not someone to be dominated. But this was when the truth struck me like a ton of bricks. All along, Willem's intentions were to push me towards greatness, using his own dragon power—that would ultimately destroy us. And yet, my heart is still his. Even now, I'm completely under his control…

The walls of Deveraux Manor seem to pulse around us, reality bending at the edges as time itself struggles to maintain this pocket of the past. Through the temporal distortion, I catch fleeting glimpses of the present—Cassandra's untamed magic spiraling, a sinister presence cutting through the crowd, Ivan's worried gaze searching for me.

Ivan. His name in my thoughts sends fresh pain through my chest. How can I feel this echo of attraction to Willem when my heart belongs so completely to another?

"My love?" Willem guides me through the candlelit halls of my ancestral home, his touch both anchor and torment. Each step feels like walking through dreams—or perhaps nightmares. The manor's familiar shadows hold different secrets in this time, before blood and betrayal stained its walls.

"Your grandmother is waiting. I believe she likes me," he says, and my heart cracks at the pride in his voice. "She says we'll make a fine match."

The portraits of my ancestors watch our passage with knowing eyes. Did they try to warn me back then? Did I miss the signs in their painted expressions, the way their frames seemed to tremble when Willem's dragon magic brushed too close?

We pause before my grandmother's study, and Willem's hand settles at the small of my back. The touch sends electricity racing through my nerve endings—muscle memory responding to a ghost. How many times did he touch me just like this, before everything shattered?

"You're quiet tonight, my heart." His voice carries that gentle concern that I'd eventually learn to distrust. But here, now, it sounds genuine. It sounds like hope.

"Just overwhelmed," I manage, and it's not entirely a lie. The weight of knowing what comes next sits heavy in my chest, making it hard to breathe. Three centuries of hindsight press against my ribcage like thorns.

"My wild little witch," Willem whispers, and his fingers trail down my neck, tracing the spot where his claiming mark should be. *Will* be. The touch sends shivers through me that I can't entirely blame on fear. "Do you know what you do to me?"

Magic arcs between us like lightning through winter skies; dragon power meeting witchcraft in an ancient, primal rhythm. His eyes darken with desire, and I remember how this hunger once seemed romantic rather than dangerous. How his need to possess me felt like passion instead of prophecy.

"I should go," I manage, but my feet won't move. The temporal bubble around us pulses with other-worldly energy, reality bending at the edges like paper too close to flame. Through the distortion, I catch fragments of the present—Cassandra being swept into Gavriil's arms, Nikolaas and Samara quietly escorting the guests away from the premises, the chaotic surge of supernatural forces colliding.

But here, in this pocket of preserved time, Willem's magic wraps around me like golden chains. Beautiful. Binding. Fatal.

"Wait," he demands, bringing us to a halt. "Just a moment more." His hand cups my face with such tenderness it makes my heart bleed. "Let me memorize you like this—innocent and perfect and mine."

The controlling edge in his voice makes something in me recoil even as my younger body leans into his touch. I want to scream warnings across time, want to tell him that love isn't ownership, that his need to contain my power will destroy us both.

Instead, I see myself rising on my toes, letting him brush his lips against mine in a kiss that tastes like destiny and damnation. His dragon magic surges, and for a heartbeat, I remember why I once thought he could make me whole.

"Thank you," I whisper against his shoulder, letting myself sink into this moment before tragedy. His arms tighten around me, and dragon magic pulses between us like a shared heartbeat. "For believing in me when even my own family doubted."

The words scrape my throat raw with memories. Willem had seen my potential when others called me difficult, dangerous, too wild to lead. He'd stood beside me at eighteen as I challenged centuries of patriarchal tradition, his dragon power lending weight to my claim as the first female head of the Deveraux line.

"Your power calls to mine," he murmurs into my hair, and I understand the truth of it even now, even knowing how this story ends. "Like recognizes like, my love. I see in you what others are too afraid to name—*a force of nature wearing human skin.*"

Moonlight spills through the gallery windows, painting us in silver and shadow as we linger in this pocket of preserved time. Through the temporal distortion, I catch glimpses of what his support will cost us both—the way his pride in my strength will curdle into possessiveness, how his desire to elevate me will become a need to contain.

But here, now, his touch carries only warmth. His dragon magic wraps around me like golden wings, protective rather than possessive. This Willem still has faith in me without needing to own me.

"You will change everything," he says, and his voice holds such conviction it makes my soul tremble. "The first of a long line of powerful women who will lead your family into a new age. And I will be there with you, watching you shine."

If only he knew how true those words would prove—and how tragic. The Deveraux matriarchy would indeed span centuries, but he wouldn't be there to see it. His love, darkened by fear and pride, would force me to choose between power and passion, between duty and desire.

I pull him closer, breathing in the scent of dragon magic and destiny, letting myself remember how it felt to love him without reservation. My tears fall silently, each one carrying the weight of centuries yet to come. His arms tighten around me, strong and sure, unknowing that this embrace carries the seeds of our destruction.

"I will love you forever," Willem whispers, his voice rough with emotion. Dragon fire dances in his eyes, pure gold unmarred by the darkness that will eventually claim him. "Our love will echo through time itself, through the joined bloodlines of Draken and Deveraux. Every generation to come will carry a piece of this magic."

His words pierce my heart like shards of prophecy. He doesn't know—can't know—how true they'll prove, how our tragic love will shape centuries of supernatural politics. How the magic born from our union will ripple through time until it culminates in Cassandra, in the impossible child she carries.

The temporal bubble shimmers around us like breaking glass, and reality begins to fracture. Willem's form starts to fade, but his last words reach me across the centuries:

"You are my destiny, Juliette Deveraux."

The time slip releases me with the gentleness of a lover's goodbye. I find myself standing in Draken Manor's moonlit courtyard, snow falling soft as memory around me. My tears freeze on my cheeks as the present reasserts itself—the sounds of chaos from the ballroom, the pulse of Cassandra's untamed magic, the weight of three centuries pressed into a single moment.

"You were wrong," I whisper to Willem's ghost, to the memory of love untainted by possession. "Destiny isn't what binds us. *Choice* is."

9

IVAN

The night embraces Draken Manor's courtyard like a lover, each snowflake a crystallized secret drifting through moonlight. I pause at the threshold, noticing Juliette as she stands unmoving amidst the swirling tempest. Her rose gold gown shimmers beneath winter's caress, tears frozen on her cheeks like diamonds carved from memory.

I read the distant look in her eyes, the way she teeters between what was and what is. Being myself a creature of centuries, I'm often tempted by these trying mind games, lured by their sweet promise of nostalgia, but haunted by the grief they bring forth.

"Found you," I say softly, letting my footsteps crunch in the fresh snow. No need for stealth—her magic has always recognized mine, even before she knew to name it love.

Juliette blinks, trying to come back to this moment, back to *me*. "Did you?" Her voice carries that edge of somewhere else, of somewhen else. She doesn't turn, but her fingers flex at her sides, gathering magic like static before a storm.

"You went far." I shrug off my coat, draping it over her shoulders. The gesture feels familiar, though I've never done it before—not in this lifetime. "The past has a strong grip tonight, ma chérie."

"The past..." She leans back against my chest, and I wrap my arms around her waist, breathing in the scent of magic and memory and moonlight. "Do you remember our first Yule together?"

"Which one?" I press a kiss to her temple. "The one where you hexed me for interrupting your ritual, or the one where I accidentally set fire to the manor's east wing?"

Her laugh breaks like winter sunrise through clouds. "The very first. Before everything changed."

"Ah." I tighten my hold, summoning back candlelight and secrets, the way her emerald eyes had gleamed with hope and possibility rather than ambition. "You wore blue velvet, and your father was convinced I'd come to steal the family grimoire."

"Instead, you stole his daughter," she breathes, white mist escaping from her blushing lips.

"As I recall, *you* did the stealing." My fingers trace patterns on her arms, following the trail of ancient magic beneath her skin. "I was merely a willing victim."

"We were so young." She turns in my embrace, and snowflakes catch in her red hair like a crown of stars. "Even you, for all your immortal years. We thought love could conquer anything."

"Didn't it?" I brush away a frozen tear with my thumb. "Here we are, three centuries later, still finding our way back to each other."

"But at what cost, my love?" Juliette's fingers trace the line of my jaw, her touch carrying echoes of other winters, other moments stolen between duty and desire. "How many pieces of ourselves did we sacrifice along the way?"

Snowflakes swirl around us like recollections given form, each one catching moonlight before dissolving against our skin. Inside the manor, supernatural chaos unfolds; but out here, time moves differently—slower, deeper, weighted with three centuries of what-ifs and almost-hads.

"I used to dream of you," I confess, pressing my forehead to hers. "In Venice, in London, in every city where I tried to forget. You haunted me like starlight —always just out of reach."

Her breath catches, a small sound that carries worlds of meaning. "And now?"

"Now I'm afraid to wake up." I cup her face between my hands, memorizing the way the evening reflects off her piercing amethyst eyes. "Afraid this is another dream, that you'll slip through my fingers like melting snow."

"Ivan..." Her magic pulses against mine, sparks of violet flickering in the soundless darkness of her widened pupils. "Everything's changing again. I can feel it—the way the past bleeds into the present, the way choices echo through time."

"Then let it change." I brush my lips across her knuckles, tasting magic and mortality and something older than both. "We're not those young lovers anymore, stumbling through the dark, hoping to find light. We've earned every scar, every memory, every moment that led us here."

Juliette's hands fist in my shirt, pulling me closer as though she could anchor herself to this moment, this reality. "Promise me," she whispers against my throat. "Promise me we won't lose each other again."

"I promise." The words emerge rough with three centuries of longing. "In this lifetime and every lifetime after. Through every choice, every change, every turn of time's wheel."

Snow continues to fall, erasing our footprints from the courtyard stones. Inside, the future unfolds in chaos and probability—Cassandra's growing power, the delicate balance of supernatural politics threatening to shatter. But here, wrapped in winter's embrace, we hold on to this moment like the precious, fragile thing it is.

"Come," I say finally, offering my arm. "Let's go save the world again."

Her smile breaks like sunlight slicing through heavy clouds. "Again? When did we ever stop?"

10

GAVRIIL

The ancient gates of Draken Manor creak open at our approach, recognizing blood and bone and legendary pride. Here, centuries of carefully layered wards wrap around us like a shroud, older and deeper than the protections my sister and I had raised at our home in Saint Petersburg. Even my bear magic stills, perceiving this place as neutral ground—*sacred* ground, where supernatural politics must bow to traditional laws.

Candlelight dances across crystal and silver, casting ethereal shadows that paint the gathered creatures in shades of myth and dignity. Emris Vaughan prowls the edges like the bear alpha he is, deceptively gentle for one who rules the British Isles with an iron grip. I respect his methods; he united warring packs through strategy, rather than bloodshed.

From my place at the head of the table, I watch Cassandra's increasing struggle to maintain control. Her power pulses against my brand in waves that grow stronger by the second, the fiercest flames flickering at the edges of her storm-grey eyes.

The crystal glasses before her slightly tremble. Frost patterns creep across the windows in shapes unrelated to Nikolaas' dragon magic. The very air around her seems to bend and twist, reality warping under the pressure of too much strength.

Beautiful. Dangerous. Mine.

But something else stirs beneath her skin, something that makes my bear bristle with recognition and uncertainty. Her scent has changed, carrying notes of ancient power that shouldn't be possible. When she shifts in her seat, trying to contain yet another surge of untamed magic, I notice the way her hand drifts unconsciously to her stomach.

The quartet in the corner begins a new piece—something modern arranged for strings that makes Samara's eyes light up. My sister throws me a pointed look across the table, a silent suggestion in her dark gaze.

"Dance with me," I say to Cassandra, rising from

my seat. The words emerge as more command than request, but gentler than usual. "Before you shatter every piece of crystal in the manor."

She looks up, defiance warring with trepidation in her expression. Another wave of preternatural energy ripples through the room, rattling the chandeliers into an ominous chime. I watch her struggle against it, the way her fingers twist in the crimson silk of her gown, how her chest rises and falls with carefully measured breaths. The brand pulses between us, responding to her growing distress with bear magic that should soothe her—but something else stirs beneath the surface, and it makes my power flare with alertness and unease.

"I don't think that's—" she begins, but I'm already offering my hand.

"It's not a request, printsessa," I all but growl, immediately softening my roughness when I add, "Shall we?"

When she rises to take my extended hand, the air around her ripples like heat waves off summer pavement. Her touch blazes along my skin, our magic tangling in archaic, inescapable currents. The scent of her—winter roses and lightning—fills my lungs, making the bear inside me pace restlessly.

Samara catches my eye as we pass, her knowing

smile carrying hints of both approval and warning. Behind her, Nikolaas' dragon rumbles in response to the gathering power, fiery frost patterns spreading across windows like frozen prophecy.

As I guide Cassandra onto the dance floor, the other dancers step back instinctively, magical creatures recognizing a force of nature in their midst.

"Breathe," I murmur, settling one hand at her waist while the other clasps her fingers. "Let the music ground you."

We move together across the ballroom floor, her body following mine through steps learned along decades of supernatural politics. But tonight feels different—the air itself seems to bend around us, reality warping wherever Cassandra's energy touches it. Each turn sends ripples of power through the gathering, making shifter magic thrum in response.

Her hand quivers in mine, fine tremors that betray the turmoil beneath her poised exterior. But the empath in me reads even deeper, picking up the fathomless uncertainty brewing in her core. My brand responds inside her, trying to restrain whatever ancient force rises within.

She slightly stumbles, and I pull her closer, my spell enveloping her like impenetrable armor. "You're fighting it too hard," I murmur against her temple.

The scent of her fills my lungs, drives my bear restless with confusion. "Let it flow through you instead."

"I can't." Her words emerge barely above a whisper, but they carry enough power to make the crystal chandeliers shudder. "If I let go even for a moment—"

"Then let go." I tighten my grip on her waist, and her magic crackles against my palm like captured lightning. "I've got you."

She looks up at me then, storm-grey eyes sparkling with violet embers, and for a heartbeat I glimpse an echo of Luciana in her defiant grace. Both of them forces of nature I tried to contain rather than understand. But where Luciana's power had been quiet strength, Cassandra burns like a star about to go supernova.

The quartet's music swells, strings weaving modern melody through classical framework, and I guide her through another turn. Her skirts flare crimson against the enchanted frost coating the windows, and my bear magic surges in response to her proximity. The brand between us pulses, stronger than ever, seeking to bridge the gap between what she is and what she's becoming.

One more burst of power rolls off her, making the very air shimmer like heat waves in winter. My spell flares to life, trying to subdue it. But her magic has blossomed beyond such simple constraints. It feels ancient now, primal—like the force that shaped stars and carved mountains.

"Look at me," I command softly, catching her chin between my fingers when she tries to turn away. Violet flames dance in her eyes, reflecting in mine like matching infernos. "Focus on my voice, on my magic. Let it guide you."

"I don't want your guidance." The words emerge sharp with rebelliousness, but her body betrays her, leaning into my touch as another surge of power threatens to overwhelm her. "I don't want—"

"What you want," I cut her off, spinning us away from a cluster of conspiratorial wolf shifters, "is irrelevant. What you *need* is control."

The music shifts, something slower now, more intimate. Around us, other couples move in careful patterns, supernatural creatures maintaining their lethal dance of politics and influence. But here, in this space, between two heartbeats, there is only us—bear and witch, brand and blazing magic.

"Of course, you'd want to control me," she murmurs, stiffening. "Did you know?" Her fingers tighten on my shoulder as another current of power courses through her. "When you branded me, did you know what I would become?"

The question catches me off guard, making my steps falter for a fraction of a second. Outside, snow descends in torrents, resonating with her power. Through the frosted windows, I catch glimpses of the Lockhart vampire watching us, his immortal gaze laden with centuries of cunningness.

"I did not," I admit, the truth tasting strange on my tongue. "I knew you were powerful, knew you carried old magic in your blood. But this..." My hand slides to her waist, sensing the force that thrums beneath her skin. "This is something else entirely."

Her expression softens, tension easing from her shoulders as she follows my lead through another turn. The empath in me grins, singing with false victory as she seems to yield. But I know better—have known since the moment I first met her. Cassandra Deveraux can never truly be tamed.

"You're different tonight," she murmurs, and something in her voice makes my bear growl in approval. "Almost... gentle."

"Perhaps the season calls for gentleness." My thumb traces circles on her lower back, pleased at how my magic swirls beneath silk and skin. The brand responds to my touch, attempting to conquer her power, to bend it to my will. But beyond that artificial harmony, I sense something far more ancient stirring. "Or perhaps you bring out the worst in me, printsessa."

She laughs—a soft, spontaneous sound that makes the chandeliers sing. "The worst?"

"The truth." I lead her through another turn, admiring her as candlelight plays across her features, painting her in gold and shadow. "You make me want impossible things."

"Like what?" The flames in her eyes slightly dim, but I'm not fooled. Her power hasn't diminished—it's merely shifting, becoming something my brand can no longer fully contain.

"Like understanding rather than dominance." The admission costs me something, but this evening feels ripe for dangerous revelations. "Like earning your trust instead of commanding it."

Her breath hitches, and for a moment, the tempestuous flow of her magic grows still. But I recognize this false peace—know it for the lie it is. My brand might whisper of submission, might paint pretty pictures of harmony and yielding, but the truth burns brighter in her eyes: Cassandra Deveraux belongs to no one but herself.

"Something's wrong." Cassandra's fingers dig into

my shoulder as new wave of power unleashes from her. Draken Manor shudders to its foundations, ancient stones groaning under the pressure of formidable strength. "Oh gods," she breathes. "Not now."

A glass shatters behind me, crystal shards tinkling against marble. Then another. The temperature plummets, my breath frosting in the air as ice spiderwebs rip through the tall windows.

Juliette's gaze meets mine across the ballroom, recognition and fear burning in their amethyst depths. She takes a half-step forward, but Ivan's hand on her arm holds her back. At the far end of the room, Samara presses closer to Nikolaas, while Vlad's silver eyes narrow with the innate wariness of a born predator. Even Clarissa Draken, usually so composed, takes an instinctive step back as the raw power filling the chamber makes her witchcraft flare in response.

"Let me help you," I murmur, catching her as her knees buckle. An incantation as dark as this demands permission and she knows that. Lightning crackles beneath her skin, magic sharp enough to taste ozone on my tongue. "Before you bring down the entire manor."

"I don't need—" Her words break off in a gasp. Above us, the chandeliers ring like crystal bells, each note carrying sufficient energy to make my teeth ache.

"Enough." I catch her face between my hands, forcing her to meet my gaze. A wine glass explodes on the nearest table, making Juliette flinch. Gasps of astonishment erupt from the surrounding supernatural horde. "Your pride isn't worth the lives in this room," I growl. "Let. Me. Help."

Violet flames burn in Cassandra's eyes as another surge of magic rips through the ballroom. The quartet's music falters, strings going discordant as her power disrupts the very air around us. Through the frosted windows, snow falls harder, mirroring the tempest building inside.

She shudders in my arms, and for a heartbeat, I think her energy is fading. Then her magic surges— not in waves this time, but in a single devastating blow that makes my bones throb with ancient power. Her spine arches, head thrown back as violet flames fully consume her eyes.

The temperature plummets. Frost races across marble floors, climbing pillars in impossible patterns. Every pane of glass in the ballroom starts to sing, crystal notes building to a crescendo that sets my teeth on edge. Something old awakens in her magic, a devastating force that tastes of starlight and endings and beginnings.

"Cassandra!" Juliette's voice barely carries over the rising keen of stressed glass.

But it's too late. Power explodes outward from Cassandra's core like a supernova, shattering every window in a cruel symphony of cracking crystal. The might of it drives us to our knees as freezing wind and snow howl through the newly created openings. Shards of glass hang suspended in the air for one impossible moment, catching candlelight and magic like a thousand prisms, before tinkling to the ground like deadly rain.

I move without thinking, wrapping myself around her, shielding her with my body as razor-sharp crystal rains down on us. My bear surges instinctively, creating a barrier of golden light, but a few shards still slice through my jacket, drawing blood.

I barely feel the cuts. All that matters is protecting her—not because she's my branded mate, not because of politics or power, but because something deeper than magic demands it. Her face is pressed against my chest, fingers clutching my shirt, and I sense the exact moment her wild force encounters my protective instinct. The brand pulses between us, but for once, it's not trying to control. Instead, it bridges our energy, bearing witness to an unexpected flash of trust.

"Gavriil, *please…*" she breathes, and the word sounds like it's being torn from her throat. "Make it stop."

I pull her closer, letting my spell enfold her in a shield. The brand flares between us, striving to contain what can no longer be contained. Behind her, Juliette takes another step forward, her own aura blazing in response to her granddaughter's distress.

"Stay back!" I command, not taking my stare off Cassandra. Her magic pulses against mine, wild and ancient and impossible. "All of you."

"She's losing control!" Juliette's voice cuts through the chaos. "Gavriil, you must—"

"I know what I must do." I keep my eyes fixed on Cassandra, even as I feel the weight of the gathering's scrutiny. Tomorrow, whispers of this night will spread through supernatural circles like wildfire. The Ursa King's branded mate, magic beyond control—they'll smell weakness, see opportunity.

Fuck that. Fuck all of it.

"Dear gods," Clarissa breathes from somewhere behind us. "Such raw power."

Another surge hits, and the crystal chandeliers sing high enough to crack. The largest one groans ominously. Metal twists with a sound like screaming steel, and the massive fixture tears free from the ceiling.

Cassandra's knees buckle completely, and I catch her against my chest. Her magic burns against my skin like arctic fire, defying every natural law. Above us, time seems to slow as the chandelier plummets toward the ballroom floor, each crystal catching fire-light one last time before inevitable destruction.

"Clarissa!" Nik's voice cuts through the chaos. In one fluid motion, he sweeps his sister out of the chan-delier's path, golden scales rippling across his skin faster than thought. His other arm catches Samara, pulling her into the protection of his embrace as his dragon armor manifests—an instinctive response to threat that transforms flesh into living gold.

The chandelier explodes against marble, shooting lethal shards of crystal in every direction. Dragon scales flash as Nik shields his charges, his wings—half-formed in the rush to protect—curling around them like an impassable fortress. The sound of shat-tering glass echoes through the ballroom like breaking fate, a crescendo to Cassandra's unleashed power.

"Brother...!" Samara's concern carries across the space between us, but I barely hear her. All that matters is the witch in my arms, the impossible storm of her magic threatening to tear reality apart.

"Focus on me," I repeat, softer now, meant for her ears alone. As her legs give way, I ease us both to our knees on the ballroom floor, cradling her against my chest. My fingers thread through her raven hair, supporting her head as violent tremors wrack her frame. Each shudder feels like it might tear her apart. "Let my magic guide yours."

She collapses further into my embrace, no longer able to hold herself upright. Through the shattered windows, snow swirls into the ballroom, dancing around us like winter spirits drawn to chaos. Her skin burns fever-hot against mine, magic racing through her veins fast enough to kindle mortal flesh. I shift to better shelter her from watching eyes, my body curving around hers as if I could absorb the storm raging within her.

Let them whisper from the shadows. Let them scheme and plot, these creatures who now see only weakness. They don't understand that true power sometimes requires surrender to find control. In this moment, nothing exists beyond the need to save her from her own devastating power—not politics, not alliances, not even my own pride.

"*Please*," she whispers again, and this time when

her eyes meet mine, I see past the violet flames to the fear beneath. "I can't hold it back anymore."

"Then don't hold it back." I ease my hand along her jawline, letting my bear magic rise fully for the first time tonight. "Let it flow into me."

The brand between us flares to life, no longer trying to subdue her power but to *channel* it. Golden light ripples across my skin as I open myself to her, letting her energy surge through me like a river finding new course. The bear inside me roars in response, primal strength meeting ancient might.

Violet and gold interweave in the surrounding air, her magic recognizing mine not as cage but as conduit. Cassandra gasps, her fingers digging into my arms as the pressure begins to ease. The fierce maelstrom of her power gradually wanes, flowing between us in patterns etched into the bones of the universe.

"That's it," I murmur against her temple. "Let your magic transform. Not destroy."

The snow swirling through the broken windows slows, then stops. The remaining crystal in the chandeliers ceases its sinister song. Even the very air seems to settle, reality no longer warping under the strain of too much power.

"*Incroyable,*" Juliette whispers as she stands on the

threshold, and I glimpse longing and revelation twining in her eyes as Ivan gently guides her inside.

Behind them, Nikolaas and Samara quietly lead the guests outside. One by one, other supernatural leaders follow, leaving us alone in the aftermath of near-catastrophe.

"You're trembling," I tell Cassandra softly, still holding her close as the last echoes of wild magic fade. Her head rests against my shoulder, exhaustion replacing fathomless might.

"So are *you*," she manages between panting breaths, her words ghosting across my skin like lacy snowflakes.

I almost smile. Even drained, she maintains that defiant edge that first drew me to her. "Perhaps we both received a lesson tonight, printsessa."

Her gaze lifts to mine then, stormy eyes now clear of violet flames. Something passes between us—not quite understanding, not quite trust, but closer than we've ever been.

"Thank you," she whispers, and for once, there's no bitterness in the words.

My arms tighten around her, pulling her near until her head rests against my chest. For a moment, I think she'll resist—she *always* resists. But exhaustion wins over rebellion, and she settles against me, her breathing gradually syncing with my heartbeat.

We stay like this, kneeling on the ballroom floor amid broken glass and melting snow. Her fingers curl into my shirt as the last traces of untamed power dissipate into the winter night. For the first time since I branded her, there's no fight between us, no battle of wills or clash of power. Just this—her weight in my arms, her magic at peace with mine, snow falling soft and silent through shattered windows.

Outside, the storm has passed. Tomorrow will bring consequences, politics, the weight of supernatural scrutiny. But for now, we've found grace in the wreckage of near-disaster. Something neither of us expected, neither of us sought, but both of us needed.

Without thinking, I press my lips to her temple, breathing in the scent of winter roses and spent lightning.

She doesn't pull away.

11

CASSANDRA

Deveraux Manor embraces us in candlelight and ancient magic, its familiar walls holding centuries of secrets. After the pandemonium at the Draken estate, the gathered supernatural elite has retreated here—neutral ground where the veil between worlds grows thin.

I huddle closer to the hearth, pulling the cashmere blanket tighter around my shoulders. The fire's warmth barely touches the bone-deep chill caused by expending so much energy. Gavriil stands nearby, close enough that his bear magic radiates heat, far enough that I don't feel caged. His dark eyes haven't left me since we arrived, watching, deliberating, knowing the truth that burns beneath my skin.

Juliette paces before her desk, the silk of her gown

rustling with each turn. She hurriedly lights candles, wards of protection, seeking to appease my inner turmoil. The others wait in the gallery—Nikolaas, Samara, Vlad—unaware of the impossible secret we harbor. Only Ivan knows, standing in the shadows like the eternal guardian he is.

"We cannot contain this much longer," Juliette says, her words meant for Gavriil. "The child's power grows stronger each day. Soon, no brand or spell will be enough."

"The others will sense it," Gavriil replies, his voice carrying that edge of possession tempered now with something resembling concern. "If they haven't already."

Magic rolls through me, gentler than before but still wild, still untamed. Steam rises where my power meets the blanket's fabric. His brand pulses in response, no longer trying to control but to diffuse, just as it did during the crisis.

"Then perhaps," Juliette says, amethyst eyes meeting mine across the space between us, "it's time to trust our allies with the truth."

The fire sputters and crackles, sending sparks dancing up the chimney. My fingers trace idle patterns on the blanket's soft weave, leaving trails of frost in their wake despite the hearth's warmth. Even now, hours after the crisis, my magic refuses to settle.

"Our allies," I repeat, tasting the words' bitter edge. "You mean Nikolaas. Samara. Vlad." My gaze drifts to Gavriil. "Your siblings, at least, deserve to know what you're protecting."

He shifts at that, firelight catching the sharp planes of his face. For an instant, I glimpse something like guilt in his expression. After all, he's kept this secret from them since the moment he perceived the child growing inside me.

"They will understand," Ivan says from his corner, speaking for the first time since we arrived. "Vladimir's disposition is noble, gentled by fatherhood, and Samara has got more heart than most give her credit for."

The Ursa King stiffens at my immortal friend's icy assessment. And yet, his silence seals approval upon each word.

"And Nikolaas?" I pull the blanket tighter as another wave of energy ripples through me. "The dragon who's about to claim her?"

"Is more invested in this alliance than you know." Gavriil moves closer, his shadow falling across me like a second blanket. Warmth radiates from him, bear magic reaching instinctively for mine. "What pertains to the Alexeevs affects *him* now."

"Everything's changing," Juliette murmurs, more to herself than us. She stands at the window, watching snow gather on the grounds. "Old alliances crumble while new ones form in their wake."

The fire flares higher as my power surges again. Without speaking, Gavriil kneels beside my chair, one hand settling on my knee. His brand pulses between us, and the reckless magic slowly loses strength.

"Bring them in," I whisper, though my voice shakes. "Before I lose my nerve."

Gavriil's hand tightens on my knee, grounding me as Ivan moves to the door. Through his brand, I sense the subtle shift in his spell—protective rather than possessive. The change still surprises me. This new understanding between us, born in disaster.

The doors slide open, bringing a rush of cooler air and the soft rumble of voices from the gallery. Samara enters first, her dark gaze immediately finding her brother beside me. Something flickers across her face —concern, recognition, acceptance. She's always been sharper than most.

Nikolaas follows, dragon magic rippling around him like invisible wings. In silence, he takes in the scene—me huddled by the fire, Gavriil's protective stance, Juliette's tense shoulders—and his ocean eyes narrow.

"Well," he says, voice dry as winter wind. "This should be interesting."

"Sit down. All of you," Juliette commands, every inch the Grand Witch despite her clear exhaustion. "What we're about to tell you cannot leave this room."

Vlad closes the doors behind them, silver gaze reflecting firelight as he leans against them. The space appears smaller now, heavy with the weight of gathered strength and unspoken revelations.

Magic surges through me again, causing the flames to dance higher. Gavriil's fingers press harder against my knee, his brand throbbing in response. "Спокойной, моя сильная," he whispers, the Russian words carrying centuries of bear wisdom in their depths. The phrase speaks directly to the power thrumming through my veins, transforming chaos into something almost musical, almost controlled.

Even when I do not speak the Ursa King's mother tongue, I've learned to recognize the expression—*be calm, my strong one*—from how often he murmurs it when my magic threatens to spiral.

I take a deep breath, unable to tear my stare from

his fierce gaze. We exchange a quick nod, silently acknowledging our mutual understanding.

When I look away, Samara is watching us with dawning realization. "You're carrying a child," she whispers, and the statement changes everything.

Silence falls heavy as snow in the study. Samara's words hang in the air like frost, delicate and dangerous. Through half-closed eyes, I watch the others process this striking declaration.

Nikolaas goes completely still, dragon energy flickering as he reassesses every interaction, every surge of energy he's witnessed thus far. Behind him, Vlad straightens from his position at the door, wolfish gaze widening with comprehension.

"A child," Samara repeats, softer now. She takes a step toward me, then stops as Gavriil's power flares in warning. "Brother..." Her stare shifts between us, sharp mind connecting pieces of a puzzle she didn't know existed. "This is why you've been so protective. Why your brand..."

"Serves a greater purpose than mere possession," he finishes, voice rough with a feeling I can't name. His hand hasn't left my knee, thumb tracing small circles that somehow help calm the magic constantly threatening to break free.

The fire dims suddenly, then roars back to life as

another wave of power rolls through me. Steam rises where my fingers clutch the blanket, frost patterns forming despite the hearth's heat.

"Not just any child," Nikolaas says, fierce eyes bright with new awareness. "A *vampire's* child."

"Dristan's," I breathe out.

The name sends fresh pain through my chest, makes my magic surge wildly enough that Gavriil has to press both hands against my shoulders to keep me grounded.

"Impossible," Vlad murmurs, but there's wonder in his voice rather than denial.

"Clearly not," I manage through clenched teeth as violet flames dance at the edges of my vision.

"A vampire-witch child." Nikolaas moves closer to the fire, his shadow scurrying across the walls like dragon wings made manifest. "The implications alone..."

"Are precisely *why* this cannot leave this room," Juliette interrupts. Candlelight mirrors in her amethyst eyes, making them gleam with centuries of carefully guarded secrets. "The wrong whisper in the wrong ear could start a supernatural war."

Samara kneels before me, ignoring her brother's low growl of warning. Her maroon eyes search mine, carrying none of the judgment I'd feared. "This is why your magic feels different," she whispers. "Like lightning trapped in a bottle, growing stronger by the day."

Another wave rolls through me, making the crystal drops on the chandelier chime ominously. Gavriil's hands tighten on my shoulders, his brand pulsing as he channels the wild power before it can explode again. The blanket slips, revealing frost patterns blooming across my dress.

"The child draws strength from both bloodlines," Juliette explains, her voice carrying that edge of ancient knowledge that still makes me shiver. "Vampire immortality meeting witchcraft in ways we've never seen before."

"And your brand?" Nikolaas asks Gavriil, indomitable might rippling around him as he processes this new reality. "How does it affect the child?"

"It doesn't." Gavriil's admission comes rough, almost reluctant. "The brand contains Cassandra's magic, barely. But the child..." His fingers flex against my shoulders. "The child's power is beyond any constraint."

The truth of it burns in my veins like arctic fire. It grows stronger each day—this impossible life inside me, taking strength from bloodlines never meant to merge.

"The question becomes," Nikolaas says. He's drawing closer, but is wise enough to keep his distance. "What happens when the child is born?"

The words send a shiver through the formidable gathering in the room. Even the flames seem to pause, holding their breath like the rest of us. My hand drifts to my still-flat belly out of its own accord, protective instinct faster than thought.

"No one knows," Juliette whispers, and for the first time tonight, I hear fear beneath her carefully maintained control. "There has never been a child like this. Vampire immortality twined with witch magic..." She trails off, amethyst eyes distant with possibilities too vast to name.

The fire dims suddenly, shadows gathering in the corners like physical guardians. Gooseflesh shoots through my being as my magic surges again. But this time, it feels different—not just power, but *purpose*. As if the child responds to our discussion of its future.

Thick silence settles in the room as the group exchange glances—not of fear, but of shared understanding.

Gradually, the oppressive atmosphere lifts like morning mist burning away. The fire returns to its languid dance, casting amber light across concerned faces that slowly ease from wariness to wonder.

"It will need protection." Samara's voice carries that fierce loyalty I've come to expect from the Alexeevs. Her hand reaches for mine, warm and steady. "From those who would fear its power, from those who would try to harness it."

"It *will* have protection." Gavriil's assurance rumbles through me like distant thunder, his hands still anchoring me to reality while magic rushes through my veins. The possessiveness in his voice has changed somehow, become something deeper than mere ownership. "The full strength of the Ursa clan stands with the child."

The words hit me like a physical force, making my power swell in response. I stare up at Gavriil, remembering that night in his study when he first scented the truth growing inside me. How his lips had curled with disdain, voice sharp as midwinter frost: *"The monster will not hinder my plans."*

But now... Now his magic wraps around me like armor, the brand no longer seeking to constrain but to defend. His hands on my shoulders radiate heat that somehow reaches past the bone-deep chill of too much power. When did this change? When did his determination to possess transform into this fierce drive to protect?

The fire catches gold in his dark eyes as he meets my questioning gaze. Something passes between us—not quite understanding, not quite trust, but deeper than either. Through the brand, I understand the shift in his spell, the way it reaches not just for me but for the impossible life that I carry. My son. Our future.

Magic washes over me again, gentler this time, as if responding to this revelation. Steam rises where my fingers clutch the blanket; but for once, the frost patterns do not spread. Even the child seems to sense this change, this new alliance born of necessity and growing into something none of us expected.

"The Ursa clan," I whisper, tasting the weight of such a promise. "You would claim him as your own?"

Gavriil's fingers flex against my shoulders, and when he speaks, his voice carries all the ancient power of his bloodline: "I already have."

The air between us crackles and shifts, magic recognizing magic in ways that transcend the brand's artificial bonds. The fire casts dancing shadows across his face, highlighting the fierce conviction in his dark eyes. For a moment, I glimpse what he must have been before loss carved him hollow—a protector, a guardian, someone who understood that true strength lies in sheltering rather than controlling.

"*And* the Drakens," Nikolaas adds, dragon magic flaring bright enough to cast new light across the study walls. His feral gaze meets mine, laden with fathomless understanding. "Any child of such power belongs to all of us now. To protect, to guide…"

"To love," Samara finishes softly, and something in my chest cracks open at the simple truth in her words. Her hand finds mine beneath the blanket, warm and steady, offering connection without demanding it. The gesture so perfectly Samara—fierce and gentle all at once.

From his position by the door, Vlad watches the scene unfold with wolfish stillness. His silver eyes reflect the firelight, carrying a predator's unique focus. But there's something else in his gaze—not just assessment, but understanding. After all, he knows what it means to love a child of mixed bloodlines, to watch power bloom in unexpected ways.

"The Volkov wolves will stand with you as well," he says finally, his voice laced with that slight Russian accent that becomes more pronounced in moments of emotion. "We know something of protecting those who bridge worlds."

His words make the magic pulse beneath my skin,

gentler now, as if the child recognizes this offer of kinship. Vlad pushes away from the door, moving with a shifter's fluid grace, and comes to stand beside his siblings. The three of them create a tableau of supernatural power—bear, wolf, and witch-born, united by blood and choice.

"Pack is more than blood," he adds softly, and I catch the way his hand drifts to the pocket where he keeps a picture of his daughter. "Sometimes, it's the family we choose to keep."

Gavriil's hold becomes iron on my shoulders. He nods, and through the brand, I sense his silent acknowledgment of his brother's wisdom.

Energy surges through me again, but this time it feels different. Instead of fighting for release, it seems to reach for the gathered power in the room—bear and dragon and wolf magic, all responding to this unthinkable new reality. The child inside me stirs, as if recognizing the vows being made, the bonds being forged in this candlelit study on a winter's night.

There can only be one father to my beloved son—Dristan. I will do everything in my power to get him back. But for now, this is enough.

12

VLAD

The magic in Deveraux Manor shifts with subtle grace, like the first whisper of spring through winter-bare branches. Through leaded glass windows, moonlight fractures into prismatic paths across fresh snow, each crystal a promise waiting to be kept. But it's not the icy wind that makes my wolf instincts stir to full alertness—something more vital approaches, something that builds the very air dense with recognition.

The gathered supernatural elite in the study takes on a different tenor as the wards ripple with acknowledgment. Gavriil's hands still rest on Cassandra's shoulders, but his dark eyes meet mine with sharp understanding. Samara's breath catches, scenting the change even as Nikolaas' dragon flares in response to this new presence.

The doors slide open, and Jon appears in the doorway, his composure slightly ruffled. "Mademoiselle, there are—"

But the words fade to insignificance as another wave of familiar energy washes through the manor. My muscles coil with the need to move, to run, to claim what's mine. Weeks of separation crystallize into this single moment of anticipation.

My gaze angles sharply, meeting my brother's stare in search of approval.

"Go," Gavriil says softly, and in that one word, I hear everything he doesn't say—understanding, permission, perhaps even envy for this kind of love that transcends politics and power.

At once, I dash through the threshold. The manor halls pass in a blur of candlelight and shadow. Behind me, the others follow at a more measured pace, their unnatural forces creating intricate harmonies in the winter breeze. But nothing matters, except the scents growing stronger with each step—vanilla and woodsmoke, milk and innocence. The unique signature of my unending joy.

The manor's grand doors swing open to wintry twilight, letting in a rush of snow—laden air that carries the fragrance of miracles. A beautiful enchantment shimmers in the space between heartbeats— *pack magic, mate magic, home.* The purest wild power that belongs only to those who run with wolves. Each breath fills my lungs with vows unbroken, with memories of summer nights and shared hunts and the quiet moments between moonrise and dawn.

"Anya," I gasp, heart throbbing hard against my chest and throat.

She stands framed in the doorway, a painting come to life, snowflakes caught in her mahogany hair like a wreath of stars. The past weeks have changed her in subtle ways—her magic runs deeper now, more controlled, the mark of a true alpha's mate. In her arms, Katya's silver eyes gleam with inherited power, small hands reaching for the snow falling around them.

"Surprise," Anya says softly, but her voice carries all the warmth of summer despite the winter chill. Her gaze meets mine across the threshold, and the bond between us pulses with recognition, with longing, with everything we've held back throughout our separation.

Behind me, I listen to Samara's quiet intake of breath, feel the shift in Gavriil's bear as he appreciates the meaning of this moment. Even Nikolaas' dragon fire seems to dim in deference to this reunion of pack and family.

"Look who's at the door," Anya softly sings to Katya, who squirms in her arms, diaphanous gaze fixed on me with fierce focus. Our child has grown— no longer the tiny cub I left behind, but a being of unspoiled magic and infinite possibility.

"Pa-pa!" my sweet daughter says.

My heart constricts, the wolf in me surging with emotions too vast to name. Endless missed moments crash over me like winter waves—first words, first steps, the way her power must have bloomed with the passing moon. Her scent fills my lungs—milk and innocence and wild magic, underlaid with an essence that is purely Katya.

"Pa-pa," she says again, and the word breaks something loose in my chest. Her small hands reach for me, energy rippling around her like invisible moonlight.

"It wouldn't be Yule without you," Anya whispers, her voice carrying all the weight of seasons spent apart, of choices made and prices paid. When she steps forward, crossing the threshold between winter and warmth, the mate bond between us throbs with all we've held back through weeks of separation.

Elated beyond reason, I gather them both in my

arms, breathing in the mingled scents of pack and home and everything that matters. Katya burrows into my neck, her magic reaching instinctively for mine, while Anya's free hand finds my heart. Snow continues to fall around us, each flake a crystallized moment of grace.

"My beautiful girls," I manage, the words rough with raw emotion. Behind us, I sense the others drawing back, granting us this instant of privacy even as their energy responds to the sheer bliss radiating through our beings.

Our reunion spills into the manor's warmth like spring thaw, pack magic tangling with the gathered power already filling these ancient halls. Samara steps forward first, her dark gaze bright with unshed tears as Katya squeals, "Sammy!" and reaches for her beloved aunt.

"There's my little wolf!" Samara breathes, gathering my Katya into her arms. My daughter's silver eyes gleam with innate magic as she pats Samara's face with small, urgent hands, sharing months of memories through touch alone—a trait unique to shifter cubs.

Gavriil maintains his distance, standing near the hearth like the alpha predator he is, but his dark gaze follows his niece's movements with carefully concealed longing. Something shifts in his expression —a softening around the eyes, a subtle change in his magic that speaks to deeper wounds than any of us fully understand.

Then Katya turns, catching sight of him, and everything changes. Her stare locks onto his with that peculiar gift wolf cubs possess—the ability to glimpse past facades to the truth lying underneath. Without hesitation, she extends her tiny arms toward him, magic rippling around her like moonlight through leaves.

"She seems to see beyond the fearsome bear," I say softly, watching as something defenseless flashes across my brother's face. For a moment, I glimpse the man he was before Sestroretsk, the brother he was before loss carved him hollow.

"Cubs often do," Cassandra adds from her place by the fire as she watches this unlikely interaction. Through her growing energy, she must sense what we all feel—the way Katya's presence seems to settle the untamed power in the room, bringing balance between forces too long at war.

The moment stretches, delicate as frost patterns, each breath weighted with unspoken opportunities. Katya fusses in Samara's hold, her tiny hands reaching for my brother.

"медведь!" *Bear*, she says, and I witness as Gavriil's carefully constructed walls begin to crack. His dark eyes keep shadows I know too well—the fear of loving anything in a world that takes so much.

"Oh, alright then," Gavriil grumbles, uncrossing his arms. "I guess I can hold you for a little while."

Behind Samara, Nikolaas moves like living shadow, all dragon grace and barely contained power. His arm slides around her waist as he whispers against her hair, soft as snowfall: "I can't wait for us to have a family of our own."

My sister's magic flares brightly, then dims, a candle caught in crosswinds. I sense her wariness— the fear that happiness might prove as fragile as winter roses. After all, we Alexeevs know too well how quickly joy can turn to ash.

Katya coos softly, nestled in Gavriil's embrace. Her intense stare sweeps the walls up to the last remnants of winter's mistletoe, hanging above, dark and dormant. Something shifts in the air then—that peculiar tension that comes in the onset of a primal force awakening. I feel it in my core.

My daughter's eyes gleam with otherworldly light as she waves her small fingers through the gathered power.

The scent hits me first—fresh green breaking

through winter's grip, impossible growth spinning from nothing.

Above us, mistletoe blooms in delicate cascades, each pearl-white berry glowing with magic that tastes of moonlight and miracles. The vines weave themselves across the dining room ceiling, creating a canopy of Yule blessing that stops every supernatural creature in their tracks.

"Impossible," Gavriil breathes, clutching Katya closer, his eyes wide with wonder.

"Not impossible," Juliette says, violet flames flickering in her pupils as she steps forward. "*Extraordinary.*" Her fingers trace patterns in the air, tracing the flow of my daughter's magic. "Witch blood flows through her veins as sure as her shifter heritage." She laughs, the sound rich with joy and delight. "Oh, the stories they'll tell of this little one!" Juliette's vampire mate materializes behind her like shadow given form, his arms sliding around her waist with practiced grace.

Anya's fingers find mine as pride swells in my chest. Our daughter, barely old enough to sit up on her own, has just woven magic that makes even the Grand Witch of the Deveraux line pause in wonder.

"ужин!" *Dinner*, Katya babbles in our mother tongue, one of her few words, but it carries all the authority of an alpha leading the pack. Within seconds, her power ripples through the manor, transforming chaos into celebration with an infant's pure intent.

"Well," Nikolaas says, dragon fire dancing in his golden eyes as he surveys the enchanted ceiling. "Since our first dinner ended rather... explosively, perhaps we should take the little witch-wolf's suggestion." His lips curve into that rare, genuine smile he seems to reserve for moments of pure delight. "After all, what better way to end a Yule evening than with family?"

13

CASSANDRA

Golden candlelight spills through the dining room's open doors, carrying bursts of laughter and the affection of unlikely fellowship. Bear and dragon, wolf and vampire—all gathered under enchanted mistletoe conjured by a child's unspoiled purpose, their ancient powers mingling like mulled wine.

As I linger in the gallery's shadowed corridor, I watch the scene unfold, a legend whispered into existence. I lean against the icy window, moonlight washing over me in pale silver streams that make my skin look faintly blue. The contrast strikes me—their radiance and my solitude, their joy and my contemplation. Through the frost-touched glass, snow falls in silent benediction, while behind me, warmth pulses from the dining room, a reminder of the unstoppable pace of life.

"Not hovering by the windows all evening, I hope?" Ivan's voice carries that unique blend of concern and sass that makes him impossible to ignore. He materializes beside me, offering a crystal glass filled with deep crimson liquid. "Though I must say, brooding does become you. Perhaps it's genetic—all Deveraux witches have a flair for the dramatic, I've found."

I eye the drink suspiciously, but he anticipates my concern with a knowing smile. "Pomegranate juice, my dearest. Enhanced with enough cinnamon and star anise that you won't feel left out of the festivities. After all," he adds, his voice softening with the tenderness he reserves for family, "you're drinking for two now."

"Solid advice from a master of mischief," I counter, accepting the thoughtful gesture. The warmth seeps into my fingers, spiced sweetness rising with the steam. "And wasn't it you who taught me the proper way to lurk in the shadows?"

His laugh sails across the gallery, drawing a few glances from the dining room where servants bustle about with steaming platters. The air fills with the scent of roasted meats and mulled spices, punctuated by bursts of laughter and animated conversation. Juliette presides at the head of the table, amethyst eyes bright with glee as she watches Samara teach little Katya to make her spoon float—her first intentional spell already leading to more.

Gavriil and Nikolaas discuss territory boundaries with surprising civility, their voices conveying hints of actual respect rather than mere political necessity. Samara leans against her dragon's shoulder, contentment softening her usual sharp edges.

My hand drifts to my belly, to the wondrous life growing stronger each day. The child's magic pulses gently now, soothed by Katya's presence in ways none of us fully understand. Through the windows, snow continues to fall, each flake carrying whispers of futures yet to be written.

But inevitably, my gaze shifts to the darkness lying beyond the glass, to the forlorn garden, where Kelham waits in shadow. His magic calls to mine across the frozen ground, ancient and knowing. I'm convinced he keeps secrets about my growing power, about the child that makes reality bend and break. And perhaps... perhaps he truly holds the key to recovering Dristan.

"Whatever you're planning," Ivan murmurs, his immortal eyes seeing too much as always, "remember… you're not alone in this." He squeezes my shoulder gently before returning to the warmth and light of the dining room.

The thought of Dristan stirs fathomless grief in my soul, but with it also comes steel-spined determination. My son will know his father. No matter what bargains must be struck, what prices must be paid. Even if it means dealing with a creature of shadow and starlight, even if it means challenging the very boundaries between our worlds.

The Ursa brand pulses against my skin as if sensing my resolve. Across the crowded room, Gavriil's dark eyes meet mine, laden with understanding rather than possession. He hardly imagines what I plan—how could he know? But for tonight, in this moment of firelight and family, I let this knowledge rest unspoken between us.

The warmth of the spiced juice seeps into my fingers as Ivan returns to Juliette's side, leaving me alone with my thoughts. Or so I believe, until a familiar presence shifts the surrounding air—cedar and smoke, power and predator.

"The party's inside, printsessa." Gavriil's voice holds none of its usual command, something almost gentle in his tone. He doesn't touch me, but his heat radiates against my back as he stands close enough that his breath stirs my hair. "Though I understand the appeal of winter's silence."

Through the window's reflection, I watch him study the dark gardens where Kelham lurks. The brand pulses once, responding to his proximity, but it feels different now—less like a leash and more like... something I'm not ready to name.

"I needed a moment," I say, the words visible as steam against the cold pane of glass. The child within me stirs, power reaching instinctively toward Gavriil's bear. "It's been a rather... intense evening."

"Mm." A sound of acknowledgment, deep in his chest. "Your magic has settled," he observes, still maintaining that careful distance. His reflection's eyes meet mine in the glass. "Something about Katya's presence seems to soothe it."

I nod, studying snowflakes as they spiral against darkness. "It's as if she reminds the power inside me that magic doesn't have to be a storm. That it can be..." I pause, searching for words to describe that which I barely understand myself.

"Pure," he finishes. "Untainted by politics or power plays." The weight of understanding in his tone compels me to turn to face him. In the dim light, his maroon eyes hold none of their usual predacious gleam—just something deep and thoughtful that transforms his entire expression.

He studies me for a long moment, choosing his next words carefully. "The child you carry..." His hand lifts, hovers near my belly without touching. "Its power will be like that too, if we protect it properly. If we let it grow into what it's meant to be, rather than what others might try to make it."

The use of 'we' doesn't escape my notice. Nor does the way his bear magic curls protectively around us both, a shield against prying eyes.

"Did you mean what you said earlier?" I ask, my voice barely above a whisper. "About protecting the child?" About accepting a vampire's son, I don't add, but the question hangs between us like frost before dawn.

"Every word." The certainty in his tone makes me look up. His gaze holds mine, utterly serious. "The Ursa clan's protection isn't given lightly, printsessa. Once promised, it's as binding as any brand." His eyes soften almost imperceptibly. "Perhaps more so, as it is freely chosen rather than forced."

A whisper of magic draws our attention upward. Fresh mistletoe blooms across the ceiling above us, white berries gleaming with inner light. Gavriil's lips curve slightly, silent wisdom stirring in his expression.

"Mistletoe," I breathe, glancing up at the green canopy.

"Our forefathers believed," he says, tone laden with an alpha's conviction, "that when two souls met beneath mistletoe, the gods themselves paused to witness their intentions. They considered it both blessing and obligation—to seal promises with a kiss, to put aside grievances, to acknowledge bonds deeper than blood or politics." His gaze finds mine again. "Even warring tribes would lay down arms under its boughs."

Heat rises to my cheeks as I realize our position—the mighty Ursa King and his branded mate, standing beneath winter's sacred plant.

Before I can respond, he moves with that liquid grace that marks him as predator. His hands glide along my jaw, tilting my face up to his. My heart thunders against my ribs, caught between instinct and intention.

"Do you accept the truce I offer, printsessa?" His voice drops to that dangerous velvet tone that makes the brand beneath my skin hum with awareness. One hand still cups my jaw, his thumb tracing the edge of my lower lip in a touch so light it might be pure imagination.

Time stretches like honey dripping from a spoon.

His breath ghosts over my lips, leaden with the aroma of bourbon and indestructible power. For one wild moment, I imagine closing that final distance, letting the mistletoe witness a different kind of promise. My eyes flutter closed, surrendering to whatever magic this instant holds.

But when his lips press against my brow instead, something shifts in my chest—relief and disappointment tangling into an emotion I'm not ready to name. It's not possession he offers with this kiss—it's harmony. Protection. A promise sealed in the old way, avowed by powers that remember when magic served unity rather than division.

I bow my head, accepting both the gesture and its deeper meaning. In this moment, we're not captor and captive, not players in a political game. We're simply two creatures standing beneath midwinter's blessing. And perhaps this is the lesson from the tales of old: that the strongest bonds aren't forged by brands or blood, but by choices made and promises kept.

EPILOGUE. IVAN

One learns to read omens after a few centuries of existence. Tonight, they whisper through falling snow, etched in frost patterns across Deveraux Manor's ancient windows. I watch the gathering from my lurking spot in the shadows—an old habit that's served me well through ages of supernatural politics.

Juliette presides over this unlikely family dinner with all the grace three centuries of waiting has granted her. My witch, my heart, finally coming into the power she was always meant to wield. Beside her, Cassandra glows with more than just pregnancy's usual radiance. The child she carries will change everything—though perhaps not in the ways any of us expect.

But it's the empty chair at our gathering that

draws my careful attention—the space where Clarissa Draken should sit. Even now, miles away, the Last Dragon Shifter's sister plays her own dangerous game, unaware of the forces stirring around her. Such a delicate thing she seems, with her pale blue eyes and careful smiles. But some fires burn brightest just before they consume everything in their path.

While we dine beneath the tides of winter, Kaisner Drachenstein plots in his Alpine fortress, weaving dragon magic through mortal crime with terrifying precision. His hunger for Nikolaas' power grows with each passing moon. And in Germany's frozen heart, a warlock climbs through criminal ranks, unknowingly moving closer to a collision that will reshape our world.

For now, the mistletoe above us pulses with cryptic power, a reminder that some magic remembers what we've forgotten. Peace *can* be chosen. Enemies can become allies. Love *can* bloom even in the heart of winter.

But beyond these candlelit windows, darkness gathers. I feel it in my immortal bones, taste it in the air like an approaching storm. The treaties forged tonight under a child's innocent magic will be tested sooner than any of us suspect.

Yet that's a tale for another time, my darling darklings. For now, let us savor this moment of grace—this gathering of formidable powers finding new ways to coexist. Let us believe, if only for this sacred season, that some bonds transcend the boundaries we create.

May your own Yuletide be blessed with such moments of magic, of possibilities unleashed, of hopes renewed. And may you remember, when winter's shadows grow long, that the strongest spells are the ones we choose to cast.

ABOUT THE AUTHOR

 Silvana G. Sánchez is the USA TODAY bestselling author of sinfully addictive dark fantasy new adult novels *Ash and Snow, Steel and Stone, Written in Blood,* and more paranormal and fantasy romance stories, including the *Vesely Academy* series. She lives in Mexico with her husband, son, and two adorable Shih-Tzus she calls her dragons. When not plotting away in her writing den, she's known to poke eyes in her practice as an ophthalmologist.

For more information:
silvanagsanchez.com
sgs.author@gmail.com